The Secrets of

Julia Hawke

BIRDCALL PUBLISHING AUSTRALIA

www.brendacheersbooks.com

First Edition

Author image Sargaison / Brisbane Headshots

Cover image © kevinruss / iStockphoto.com

ISBN-13: 978-0-9924287-8-5

There is a stone house in Greece where I stayed whilst planning this story. The desk was made from an old olive oil vat. I wish I were there now.

The Secrets of
Julia Hawke

Brenda Cheers

CHAPTER ONE

"I can't wait to get out of here." Julia's fingers were tapping on the handle of her suitcase. She'd said this to no-one in particular, but several people around her nodded. The woman holding the baby, the newborn dressed in blue who had been bawling almost non-stop since Dubai, was rolling her eyes. The baby was now asleep.

The aerobridge was crammed with passengers escaping the torturous flight. Julia was jostled as she fought for space. She knew that rushing was useless—there would still be queues at the immigration counters.

The flight attendant smiled in sympathy as she saw Julia emerge. "You survived Economy Class, then!"

"Barely."

"Welcome home, anyway."

Julia thought of buying cigarettes in the Duty Free store, even though she'd quit months before—a reflex action that she had the urge to give into. It was only the crowded counters that deterred her. She could always buy a pack after she left the airport.

Julia clutched a priority voucher for customs and immigration tightly in her hand. She had glimpsed it poking out from the pocket of a business-class seat, and had scooped it up as she made her way to the front of the aircraft. Even with this voucher, she had to wait in a queue, and spent that time fanning herself with her passport.

Finally she broke free of the formalities and through to the public arrivals area. She scanned the faces, feeling her stomach squeeze when she thought nobody was there to meet her. A tall figure stepped forward. "Mum!"

"Thank God. I thought no-one had come." She raised herself on the balls of her feet to kiss Costas on the cheek. Her son's lack of reciprocation gave a clue to his mood. She chose to ignore it.

"How much luggage do you have?"

"None. Just what I've got here."

Costas took the rolling case and backpack from Julia and began striding through the terminal. Julia followed him, almost at a run. She shivered as they crossed over to the car-park. Costas stood before a machine and inserted a parking ticket. Julia pulled her purse out of the pocket of her jacket. "Here."

Costas shook his head and fed notes into the slot. As soon as the ticket was re-issued he began striding again, only stopping when he reached the antique convertible.

"Wow. Your father lets you drive his most treasured possession? I'm impressed."

Costas slammed the boot closed. His eyes met hers and their expression was anything but friendly. "C'mon. Get in."

He drove in silence until they entered the Airport Link Tunnel. Costas adjusted his mirrors slightly. "Where were you? We were trying to find you everywhere. You didn't even tell us you were going overseas."

"It was a sudden decision."

"Where were you?"

"A few different places. Rural France mostly."

"Did Peter know?"

"Of course."

"You've got no idea what trouble this has caused. Elizabeth and Catherine are really upset."

"I didn't mean for that to happen. How was I to know?"

"Why didn't you tell us? Was it another man?"

"No! Why would you think that?"

Costas turned and looked at her. "You do have a history—"

"Oh, for heaven's sake. That was years ago. Watch where you're going."

Costas turned back to look at the road. His brow was furrowed. "So? Tell me."

"I had to go and do some things. Personal things."

"Secrets again, huh? I'm still not old enough to know?"

Julia looked out her passenger side window at the tunnel sections flashing by. "No, you're old enough. But it's personal."

"Home or hospital?"

"I'll call in at the hospital first. He's still unchanged, I take it?"

"It's about time you asked. Yes, unchanged."

"I spoke to the specialist while transiting in Dubai. He said there would be no change for a long time."

Costas grunted and indicated for a right exit from the tunnel. "I'll drop you and keep going."

"I was hoping you'd show me which ward he's in."

"Nup. Gotta keep going."

"This hospital is like a rabbit warren."

"Yup."

"Okay, I guess I'll find it. What's Nicholas up to?"

"Studying for exams. They're soon."

"I'll call him after I've seen Peter."

Costas pulled in to the curb, his eyes not leaving the windscreen. "Bye. I'll take the luggage to your house."

"Thanks for picking me up. I'll see you soon?"

Costas shrugged. Julia stepped onto the footpath, and as soon as she closed the car door, Costas accelerated back into the traffic.

Julia shivered in apprehension as she approached the hospital information counter. "I'm looking for Peter Howard."

The woman tapped a keyboard. "He's in ICU." She gave instructions which seemed terribly complicated to Julia, who wrote them in a notebook.

As she got close to the ward, she saw a waiting area to the left. A young woman was standing in the doorway. "Julia!"

"Elizabeth! How is your father?"

"Awful. Really bad. Where have you been?"

"Overseas. I came back as soon as I heard."

"We were trying to contact you for ages."

"Sorry. There was no mobile phone reception."

"For that long?"

"Tell me about your father."

Another figure emerged from the waiting room.

"Hi Julia."

"Catherine. Hello."

"Where have you been? We were going mad trying to find you."

"Yes, sorry. I was just telling Elizabeth—"

"We didn't know what to do."

"Yes, well, I'm back now."

"Did Dad know where you were?"

"Of course he did, Catherine."

"The doctor said he's so much worse because there wasn't anyone with him when he had the heart attack. He was all alone." Tears welled in the young woman's eyes.

"Well, we didn't know it was going to happen, did we?" Julia's patience was being limited by tiredness. "I've come straight from the flight. I'd just like to see your father and then go home and change."

"You can't see him now. They're doing something to him."

"Like what?"

"Oh, I don't know. Something to do with the breathing tube I think. They had to intubate him when they first brought him in."

"Yes, the doctor told me."

"Did he tell you how long Dad might be like this?"

"Yes. So I can't see him now?"

"Maybe if you wait."

The three women moved into the waiting area and sat down. The room was otherwise empty, and they sat apart, Elizabeth on a chair opposite Julia, and Catherine a few chairs along from her sister. Peter's two daughters were now in a position to watch Julia closely, like a prisoner being interrogated. Elizabeth spoke first.

"So where did you say you were?"

"Overseas."

"Costas and Nicholas didn't even seem to know where you were."

"No, it was a sudden trip."

"Who were you with?"

"I was travelling alone."

"Why?"

"Personal reasons."

Catherine frowned at her. "You're not going to tell us, are you?"

Julia collapsed back into her chair. "Does it matter? What has happened, happened. There is no changing it. I'm sorry your father was alone when he had his heart attack, okay?" She stood and brushed her clothes. "I'm going to catch a cab home to change. I'll talk to you both later."

There was a stunned silence as she walked out the door. No fake kisses or forced niceties. The old Julia, the one who always kept the peace, who was unfailingly friendly and accepting, was gone. The new one felt a hell of a lot better.

"So what's naughty Julia been up to then?"

Julia smiled into the mobile phone. Her brother could always make her feel better. "Oh, you know— leaving the country before my man was about to have a heart attack, and causing everyone great bother."

"And I bet you did it on purpose too, just to show those catty daughters of Peter's what a real bitch you are!"

"True! Oh, it's good to hear a friendly voice."

"So what's the story? How's Peter?"

"In ICU. In a bad way. Doesn't sound like he'll recover fully."

"They always say that."

"Hmm. You might be right. Hang on—I'll just pay the driver." She held out a credit card and waited for the transaction to be processed. "Back again."

"Mum and Dad are wondering why you took off overseas without telling them."

"Yeah, I'll give them a call. There were just things happening—"

"Sounds like you need a friend. Where's Raz these days? I can't remember seeing her for years."

"We sort of lost touch."

"Shame. You two were as close as peas in a pod."

"You know that none of my men have ever liked her—hated our friendship. Peter in particular."

"All the more reason to stay close to her. Peter would have felt threatened by her lifestyle and how close you were. Why don't you give her a call?"

Julia walked to her front door. The case and backpack were lying neatly to one side. She fumbled in her pocket for the keys to the house. "Yes, I guess I could. I reckon she'd still be angry with me, though."

"She'll forgive you."

The front door swung open, and Julia gasped. The inside of the house was a testament to the emergency that had taken place in her absence. Wrappings of a medical nature were strewn all over the floor. "You should see the mess in the house."

"Well, it would be beneath Elizabeth and Catherine to clean it up. That would fall in the category of niceness."

"They probably didn't think—"

"I bet they've been in and out of the house getting stuff for their father. Would leave the mess as a sign of protest. Nasty girls."

Julia sat down on the sofa and rubbed her forehead. "I just don't know where to start. I have to call in at the café and see what's happening."

"Not right now. You probably need sleep after the flight. Where did you come from today?"

"Today? You mean two days ago. It started in rural France. Bordeaux to Gatwick, transfer to Heathrow. London to Dubai. Dubai-Sydney-Brisbane."

"Yuck."

"And although I had a business class seat booked for my return later in the month, I couldn't use it because there weren't spare seats. Was down the back next to a screaming infant."

Christopher laughed. "Oh shit."

"Indeed."

"I'll let you go and shower or rest or something. Call me if you want to discuss your secret."

"Oh, it's not really a secret—"

"Yes it is because you're not telling anyone. You've always been like that."

"That's not fair!"

"But true. Even better, call Raz."

"I'll think about it. Thanks for the call."

"No probs. Take care and keep me posted on how Peter is. Okay?"

"Sure."

She looked around her in defeat. Unpacking, cleaning, showering, hair and makeup. It was all too hard. She lay her head on the arm of the sofa and reached blindly for the merino blanket that was always folded across the footrest. She fell into a deep sleep.

It wasn't until she woke at a little after two in the

morning—jet-lagged and disoriented—that she realised the house was empty except for her. Peter wasn't there and wouldn't be in the foreseeable future. She moved her head from side to side to relieve a kink in her neck, then lay her head back on the arm of the sofa and stared upwards. She was wide awake. Enough light was entering from the street for her to see that spiders had decorated one corner of the ceiling, and she resisted the urge to sweep the webs down immediately.

She wriggled her body until it was comfortable again and stared back at the ceiling. How did she feel? Numb. Would she miss Peter? She would likely miss his presence in the house. Would Peter need her undivided care and attention when he eventually came home? She shuddered at the thought.

The café. How had it been functioning in her absence? She'd heard nothing despite leaving instructions for weekly reports. Before she'd lost mobile access, she'd sent texts and tried to call Barry. What was he up to? She'd better turn up at opening time to check.

Nicholas was studying for his year twelve exams—an important time. She'd need to speak to him as soon as possible. Her parents as well. It was a wonder her mother hadn't tried to call. It was a wonder her mobile hadn't rung continually since she returned.

Frowning, she reached over to the back of the sofa, where she'd thrown her jacket, and retrieved her mobile telephone. The screen was blank. She tried pressing the power button, but nothing happened. Damn. She swung her legs onto the floor and walked into the study, where she knew there was a charger. She connected the device and looked around her. Mess. Peter was never a tidy man, but he'd outdone himself in her absence. Books and papers were strewn all over the floor.

He always used a special type of notebook: A4 Cashiers, French paper. It was open to the most recently-used page where there was an itemised list. The last entry was in capital letters, and she could see he'd pressed heavily with his fountain pen nib. It said, "FIX LIVING ARRANGEMENTS!"

Julia nodded. It had come to that, then.

CHAPTER TWO

The parking attendant smiled and waved. Julia opened her window. "Hello Jim. Got a spot for me?"

"Mornin' Julia. Nice to see you back. Things have been bloody dull around here without you. Love your hair. Just over there on the right should be good for now. Leave me the keys, though."

"Sure, but my hair is awful." She parked in the spot he had pointed to. As she handed him the keys, she had a thought. "Tell me what's been going on. Seen anything of Barry?"

Jim looked down at the floor. "Um. No. Not lately."

"C'mon Jim. You and I—we're old friends. Tell me what's going on."

"He buggered off."

"What?"

Jim shrugged. "Stopped turnin' up. One of the girls said he got a phone call and just bloomin' walked out."

Julia seemed unable to find any words. "So..."

"So, the girls tried to cope on their own, but it was too bloody hard. They found someone to fill in. Irishman. Funny guy."

"I don't believe it." She stood shaking her head.

"Best you go and see for yerself."

"Yes, I suppose so. Thanks, Jim. You're a good friend."

The elevator ride to the lobby seemed interminable. As soon as the doors opened, Julia rushed out and ran around to where the café stood. It was vacant. She checked the time on the lobby clock and sighed. There was still half an hour until opening time.

She raised the security grill and reached under the counter for the takings book. It wasn't there. She looked in cupboards and between shelving, but the ledger remained elusive. She was down on haunches when a voice, a close one, made her bob up suddenly. She hit her head on a cupboard door.

"Well, what do we have here, then? A coffee thief?"

"No, I—". She looked around and saw a scruffy young man surveying her with laughing eyes.

"You'd be Julia, then." His Irish accent was disarming. Julia found herself smiling.

"Yes. And you are?"

"Steven." He held out his hand and shook hers gently. "The best barista in the world."

"And modest, too."

"Oh yes. I totally under-rate my talents."

"You may be able to solve a mystery—"

"The missing ledger, is it?" He reached into his worn backpack. "I took it home to do some analysis."

"Oh?"

"The centre managers have been circling. Talking about a rent review. Wanted me to tell them how to get in touch with you."

Julia pushed some hair from her forehead. "Well, that isn't good news."

"No, I didn't think so. I told them they'd just have to wait until you got back."

He stowed his backpack under the counter and moved to the storeroom. Soon he was placing chairs and tables around the lobby area, whistling an upbeat tune. Julia stood and watched, biting her bottom lip.

"And the girls...?"

"Trudy asked for time off to study for exams. Becki is due in soon."

"Can you cope with just Becki?"

He shrugged. "I've had to for the past week. At least you're back now."

"My partner, Peter. He had a massive heart attack while I was away. He's in intensive care."

Steven stopped moving the furniture and looked at her. "No. Be damned."

"Yes. So I'm not going to be much use to you in the short term. In fact, I have to go to the hospital next. I haven't seen Peter since I got home." Steven was nodding. "But I'll see if I can get someone to help you and Becki." She began uncovering machines and arranging cups and saucers.

"No, Julia. Leave that. We'll manage. If you can find someone else, well and good. Otherwise, we'll just do it ourselves."

Julia looked into the kind eyes of this stranger and felt tears welling. She turned and picked up her bag. "Thanks, Steven. I'll be back later. We'll have a chat."

She stuffed a pile of mail into her bag, along

with the ledger and headed to the elevators, wiping her eyes as she did so. A rent review on top of everything else? That'd be damned right.

The voice at the other end sounded bored. "Hey Mum."

"Hey yourself. Studying hard?"

"Yup."

"Think you'll do okay?"

"Yup."

"Great. Sorry I've been out of touch."

"No probs. Where did you go? People were going mental."

"Yeah, tell me about it. I just had to go overseas, but I'm back now so it doesn't matter."

"Oh, okay."

"Do you want to come to my place for dinner soon?"

"Sure, but I'd better check with Dad."

"Of course. Let me know, okay?"

"Yeah. Gotta go."

"Fine. Love you." The mobile went dead in Julia's ear. She realised she'd been shivering, and that there was a westerly wind racing down the street next to the hospital. She hurried inside and up to Peter's ward.

She felt herself tensing as the waiting area came into view. There were people inside, but Peter's daughters were nowhere to be seen. She walked past to the area where the critical patients were kept, stopping at a nurses station. There were signs indicating she must wait before proceeding past that point. Other signs listed the hygiene routine that had to be undertaken when she was granted access. She was reading these when a nurse appeared.

"Julia, is that you?"

Julia turned and looked at the woman without comprehension. Then realisation dawned.

"Amanda? Do you work here now?"

"Yes. It's great to see you." Her face took on a look of sympathy. "Who are you here for?"

"My partner, Peter Howard."

"Oh, gosh. I'm sorry. I didn't realise he was your guy. How long have you been together?"

"Oh, nine—nearly ten years."

Amanda frowned. She took Julia's elbow and led her away from the desk.

"There's someone in there who says she's his wife."

Julia snorted. "That'd be right. And two daughters?"

"Yes. They've almost set up camp here since he was brought in. They didn't mention you."

Julia stared at the other woman for several seconds until she felt she could speak coherently. "I've been overseas and didn't have mobile phone signal..."

"Oh, I see. So, if you and Peter have been together all that time, who is she?"

"I guess she's still his wife. He's never gotten around to a divorce."

Amanda raised her brows. "I see." She looked around into the patient area. "I have to move those women out anyway. There aren't meant to be that many visitors at one time. I'll tell them you're here wanting to see him."

"Thanks, Amanda."

"You might want to, I don't know, go to the waiting area?"

"Yes, of course."

Minutes went by before she heard footsteps

and voices approaching. One voice, high and strident, drowned out the others. "I don't care. He's still my husband. If that bitch..." Julia covered her ears and turned away from the waiting room door hoping they wouldn't enter. A woman, sitting close by, clicking knitting needles, looked at her with interest.

Someone touched her elbow. "It's all clear, Julia." Amanda was smiling. "She's a piece of work, that ex-wife of his. Come through and see your Peter."

"What can you tell me about him, his condition?"

"Have you spoken to the specialist?"

"A couple of days ago when I was in transit."

"It's not good, I'm afraid. One of the daughters found him, and no one knows how long it had been since the attack. She called an ambulance, but his heart had stopped, then she witnessed him stop breathing. The ambulance arrived as quickly as possible, but..."

"Yes, the specialist said that."

They approached a bed that was surrounded by machines. Peter had a mask strapped to his face, and as a machine made a sound, his chest expanded.

"You can talk to him and give him a kiss."

"Will he know?"

"Maybe, maybe not, but it never hurts."

Julia squeezed Peter's hand, the one closest to her that had a needle in the vein at the top. She did this carefully so as not to upset the equipment. "Hello Peter. I'm home." She watched for a sign of recognition, but there wasn't one.

Amanda was doing something with the machines. "Don't be frightened. Give him a hug if you want."

"No. I won't do that. Thanks anyway."

Amanda looked at her and nodded. "I can't tell you much more. He's comfortable. When he regains consciousness we'll be able to assess the damage." She looked at a chart at the base of the bed. "He's almost seventy?"

"Yes. A lot older than me."

"It's funny to think that we were once schoolgirls, our whole adult lives ahead of us. Mrs. O'Brien used to tell us that. Remember?"

Julia smiled at the memory. Their English teacher was prone to lecturing them about making the most of their lives ahead. "She used to tell us to make sure we took control of our lives before someone else did it for us."

"She was right." They laughed quietly. "You did okay, you and Rachel. You didn't let anyone tell you what to do. Went off and had adventures."

"Yes, we did okay back then. Raz—she's still a free spirit. I got bogged down."

"You married the Greek guy. I met him at the class reunion."

"Yes. Had two boys, Costas and Nicholas. The marriage lasted ten years."

"Then you got together with Peter here."

"After a while. There was someone in between, but it didn't work out. How about you? You were still single last time I saw you."

"Still am. I have my dogs and a career. Works better."

The women smiled at each other, their brief joint history creating a bond.

Julia looked back at Peter. "I feel there's not a lot I can do here."

"It's natural that you'd feel that way. You can stay for as long as you like, though."

"I just—I'm not like that. I don't want to sit here for hours and watch a machine help him breathe."

"No-one's saying you should. You have a business, don't you?"

"Yes, a coffee shop that needs my attention desperately."

"Go, then. Let Peter's daughters do the minding. They obviously have more spare time than you."

Julia smiled gratefully. She'd just been handed a Get out of Jail Free card. She squeezed Amanda's arm. "Thanks for that."

"No problem. Give me your mobile number. I'll let you know if anything changes." As Julia rattled off the number, Amanda made a note on the chart. "Done. Go!"

"Thanks!" She looked at Peter again. "Bye for now." As she left the ward, her mind was already running through the next items on the to-do list.

"Trudy speaking."

"Hi Trudy, it's Julia."

"Oh, hey! You're back. How was the trip?"

"Okay, but there was an emergency back here. Peter had a heart attack."

"No! I'm so sorry."

"Which is the reason for the call..."

"Yeah?"

"I really need you back at the café. Steven and Becki are having trouble coping and I can't be there much."

"No, gee I'm sorry. I can't Julia. As much as I'd like to help out. These exams are too important. I'm studying 24/7."

"Do you know anyone else who could fill in?"

"Not offhand, but if I think of anyone..."

"Thanks. Hey, tell me what happened to Brian."

"Oh, yeah. That was weird. He got a call on his mobile and strode around the foyer talking and waving his arms. He hung up and walked towards Becki and me with a really angry look on his face. He untied his apron, handed me the keys, and walked off. That was the last we saw of him."

"Did you try calling?"

"He wouldn't pick up."

"Damn."

"Steven's great, though. A better barista. The customers love his accent."

"Thanks for finding him. Do you have his details anywhere?"

"Yeah, a copy of his references are in the back of the takings book."

"Good. I'll have a look at them. Does he intend to stick around?"

"You'll have to ask him that. He was a bit vague on that subject. We just needed someone in a hurry and he was there."

"Okay. I'll try not to disturb you any more before your exams, but if you think of anyone..."

"Sure."

"Good luck."

"Thanks. And I hope Peter recovers quickly."

As Julia finished the call, she leaned her head on the steering wheel and closed her eyes. She still had to see her parents, and wondered if she could persuade either of them to help out in the café. She didn't like her chances.

"So why don't you get in touch with that strange friend of yours? That Rachel person." Her mother almost sniffed at saying her name.

"I haven't spoken to Raz in a long time, Mum. Years."

"Well, I can't say it's a sad loss, but if you need help you should call her. At least she knows how to run the café." Julia's mother slid the tin of biscuits across the bench-top, and Julia slid them back.

"Yes, she'd be a bonus. But if you and Dad—"

"No. Your father isn't well. Then there's me and I can't stand for very long. You know that."

Julia knew her mother was as strong as an ox when she wanted to be, but she was also as stubborn as a mule. Julia was wasting her time.

"Where is Dad, anyway?"

"At his club. He's been spending a lot of time there lately."

"I thought you said he wasn't well."

"That's what he tells me. Says he's not sleeping. Gets cramps and things. Always cranky."

"Until he goes to the club?"

Julia's mother frowned as though this thought hadn't occurred to her before. "Now that you mention it..."

"Don't worry about that now." Julia thought it prudent to change the subject. Besides, her tolerance was beginning to wane. "I've got to keep going." A thought came to her. "Dad knew I was coming, didn't he? You did tell him."

"Yes, but you know him. He can be a bit funny at times."

Julia frowned. "You mean he went to his club to avoid seeing me?"

"It'll pass. He just got—well—he threw one of

his hissy fits."

"About me? What did I do now?"

"Well, you know. Going off like that and not being there when Peter had his attack."

"I didn't know it was going to happen! I didn't do it on purpose."

"Not telling us you were going—"

"Christ, that's so unfair! He could have given me the benefit of the doubt." She felt tears of self-pity welling. "Anyway, I have to go."

"Why? You only just got here. You haven't told me anything about this mysterious trip of yours." Her mother peered over her glasses, looking at Julia closely. "Wasn't another man was it?"

"No! Why has everyone jumped to that conclusion?"

"Why indeed! Maybe because you have a history—"

"Once. I did it once. It doesn't mean I'm going to make a career of it!"

"You cared little enough about your marriage back then that you threw it away, and for what? You didn't even stay with that Chinese man. What was his name?"

"He wasn't Chinese! Where did you get that idea?"

"He was living in Hong Kong?"

"Sent there for work. Philip was Australian with English parents. Anyway, that's history now."

"And now you've got that lovely Peter. What a nice man! I feel awful about his heart-attack."

"He feels worse about it than you do."

"I suppose you'll have to nurse him when he gets home. What will you do about the café then?"

"I'm just taking things one problem at a time. I

can't afford to hire anyone else."

"Anyway, if it wasn't another man, why the secrecy about your trip?"

"I just had to attend to some personal matters."

Julia's mother grunted and turned away. "Personal matters, my foot. You're hiding something."

"I have to get back to the café, Mum. We'll talk again later." She stooped to kiss her mother on the cheek. "Take care. Give my love to Dad."

Clouds had been gathering while she was visiting her mother. As she drove toward the city, drops of rain began appearing on her windscreen. The wiper blades juddered across her vision, reminding her they needed replacing. That small fact seemed to cause a dam to burst.

She pulled over to the side of the road and rested her head on the steering wheel. Soon she was sobbing—huge, wracking sobs that made her whole body shake. She was conscious of cars and trucks speeding past her, making the small sedan rock. A headache began, an insidious, stabbing pain. She tried to calm herself by breathing deeply until her heartbeat returned to normal. The headache eased.

She rummaged in her bag to find the mobile phone. The specialist's number was stored, so she selected it with shaking fingers.

"Dr. Cavendish's rooms."

Julia frowned. She didn't know this voice. "Oh, hi. This is Julia Hawke. I need to make an appointment to see the doctor."

"He has no appointments available for five weeks."

"Oh? I've been away. He told me to see him as

soon as I got back."

"Well, I'm afraid he can't see you until, hold on. Let me check."

"Could you please contact him and see if he wants to see me any earlier?" There was no response. The woman had put her on hold. Julia disconnected the call angrily.

The screen on her mobile returned to her contacts. Julia scrolled through until she saw the entry for Raz. The contact record included an image, and it showed a woman crossing her eyes and poking her tongue out. Her hair was multi-coloured. Julia smiled. Darling Raz. What she wouldn't give to see her right now. Raz would have the answers to all her woes. She always did.

Julia's finger hovered over the telephone symbol. She held it there a few seconds while biting her lip. Would her friend forgive her? Raz had been puzzled when Julia had given her the cold shoulder, continually asking what was wrong until they'd had a terrible row. Things were said. Raz had accused Julia of being a cold bitch.

Although Raz calmed down and apologised, it had been convenient for Julia to stay angry with her. It made it easier to force the necessary break.

Raz eventually had stopped calling. Julia felt her face become hot at the memory. It had been an awful thing to do, and for what? To keep the peace with Peter? She shoved the mobile phone back into her bag, an action fuelled by self-disgust.

The section of highway Julia had pulled up on was busy, and it took minutes before she could merge back into the traffic flow. She thought about what action to take next. She began yawning and found that her eyelids were closing of their own accord. Damned jet lag. She turned the radio volume up to high and drove until she reached the highway exit that would eventually lead to her house.

CHAPTER THREE

A soothing melody pulled Julia out of sleep. It was the alarm on her mobile telephone, the tune selected for its gentleness.

Only an hour had passed since she'd set the timer and fallen into a deep sleep. More sleeping time would have upset the recovery from jet lag, and she wanted to return to the café to help with closing. She needed to talk to Steven. Needed to look at his references. Needed to look at the takings versus bank balance. She sighed.

After smoothing her hair and carefully applying lipstick, she drove back into the city. Jim wasn't manning the car park, but she found a space not far from the entrance. As the elevator doors slid apart, she heard a man's voice.

"Julia, my darling! Oh, my heart beats faster! You've returned to me."

There was a flurry of activity as the man strode from the elevator and folded Julia in a bear hug. He smelled of expensive cologne and hair product. He pushed her out to arm's length and examined her closely.

"Hmm. We've lost weight, have we? I don't think you needed that, darling. Looking a bit drawn in the face. And the hair! You'd better get yourself in front of Oscar rather quickly, hey?"

Julia was laughing. "Yes, yes. I'm a mess. I know that."

"And your nails! A manicure, darling."

"Soon. Things are a bit—"

"No excuse. I heard about Peter. It caused a great kerfuffle in chambers, of course. Much wailing and weeping. Beating of breasts. You know."

"I can imagine."

"But that's no excuse to let yourself get tacky, darling."

"You're quite right." She looked fondly at Damien. He acted quite gay, but was known as a lady-killer. He would always flirt with her outrageously when she served him coffee. "I'll get myself sorted immediately!"

"Good girl. On the way to the coffee shop? That Steven is popular with the girls."

"The Irish accent?"

"Hmm. And the scruffy, unkempt look. Seems to bring out the nurturing instinct. I've been thinking of taking it on myself."

"You? Scruffy? That I'd like to see!" The two of them laughed. The elevator doors opened again and Jones, head of chambers, emerged. He looked at Julia and frowned.

"Julia? Didn't expect to see you laughing while Peter is at death's door."

Julia pursed her lips. "No, not near death.

Holding his own."

"I thought you'd be by his bedside. Where have you been, by the way? You set off quite a search, caused a lot of people a lot of trouble."

"Peter knew where I was."

"Yes, but he couldn't tell us. So?"

"Away. I had to attend to some personal matters."

"I see." Jones stared at her over the top of his glasses. "So what is the report from Peter's specialists today?"

"I haven't seen them today."

Jones gave a sudden intake of breath. "Yesterday, then?"

"I'll be seeing them tomorrow. If you'll excuse me, I have to go upstairs."

"Yes, well, you'll keep me informed." Jones strode off towards his car. Damien was shaking with suppressed laughter.

"You are such a naughty girl. That's why I like you!"

Julia hit Damien on the arm and then pressed the elevator button, hoping to avoid any more of Peter's colleagues.

"Will you be having a coffee yerself then, Julia?"

"That would be marvellous, Steven. Thanks so much."

Becki was cleaning equipment furiously, avoiding Julia's gaze. She'd been hostile since Julia's arrival, only answering her queries with monosyllabic replies. Julia's request that Becki close the café while she caught up on business matters with Steven was met with an angry silence.

"Don't worry about her. She's been working hard." Steven was leaning forward, whispering. "She'll come good. Any luck in finding someone to help?"

"No, but I'm still trying. Leave it with me. Hey, but when I'm working here, I can't carry cups of hot liquid. Not at the moment."

"That's hard in a coffee shop." Steven smiled. "What's the problem?"

"Just a weakness in my arms that comes on suddenly. Hopefully it's just temporary. I'll be best at taking orders and receiving money."

"Sure. That would be a huge help, anyway."

They spoke about takings and banking. Fortunately the takings hadn't dropped while she'd been gone. "But the rent is overdue. I thought yer might want to take care of that."

"Yes, thanks Steven. I hope you're planning to stay with us for a while?"

The Irishman shrugged. "I don't usually make long-term plans. Just travellin' around, yer know? There's not much to keep me in Brisbane." Julia's face must have shown despair. Steven smiled and took her hand. "I won't leave yer dangling Julia. Let's see how things go for the next few weeks."

"Thanks. It means a lot to me." She took a sip of coffee. "Wow. You make a mean brew."

"Like it?"

"Indeed!"

Steven's face lit up. "The lawyers seem to like it as well."

"And they are hard to please."

"So your man is one of them?"

"A barrister. Yes."

"There's another, Damien. Was asking about you all the time."

"The flirt? Yes, I just saw him downstairs."

"Lots of people were asking about you. Then there's the ones about the rent review."

"I suppose I'll have to deal with them next."

"Leave them danglin' for a while. It won't hurt."

"I just don't think this café will survive an increase."

"That's the thing you see. Them saying they will review the rent just says they're opening the subject for negotiation."

"Really? In the past it has meant an increase."

"Only if yer don't play your cards right."

"Really?"

"Another thing, too. You could raise yer prices."

"You don't know these people—these law firms. They're always complaining."

"Take no notice. I know how you spoil them. The bald guy still expected his special French treats while you were away. The Greek pastries for the hairy guy. Where else would they get such treatment?"

"I don't know..."

"Then the way they expect deliveries of coffees for meetings, at short notice. Who else would do that?"

"Maybe you're right."

"Anyway, I told you I took the takings book for analysis. There are a few things I think we should try."

Julie must have looked doubtful.

"I'm qualified. I have an MBA."

"Really? Wow!"

"Don't look so surprised." He laughed. "Just find another worker to help Becki and me, and let me try a few things, okay?"

"Alright."

"And when it comes to the rent review, let me handle it. I'll go for a rent reduction to start proceedings."

"You're a treasure. Thank you."

"Yer more than welcome."

That night, while wide-awake with ongoing jet lag, Julia sat with a notebook. She was trying to make sense of her situation—trying to find her exact position again in the world.

People close to her were causing confusion. Others who really belonged on the periphery of her life were being allies. She drew a line down the middle of the page and wrote headings, "Supporters" and "Detractors".

The detractors came to mind more readily because they were surprising. She scribbled their names quickly: Mum, Dad, and the elder of her sons, Costas. Not surprising were Peter's two daughters, Elizabeth and Catherine. Others that she'd felt hostility from were Jones from chambers and Becki the waitress.

The supporters warmed her heart. They were her brother, Christopher, who had been non-judgmental and supportive his whole life. Alison, the ward-sister who she went to school with, was also warm and helpful. Jim in the car-park. Steven the barista. Damien the flirt. These were all people that she could count on to some degree or another, even if it was for a friendly smile and hello.

She didn't know under which column Raz now belonged, and wondered if it was time she found out.

What about Peter? Friend or foe? Just because they had been having relationship issues didn't mean he was now the enemy. It just felt that way, because it seemed she might now be trapped into nursing him.

As she was noting down these thoughts, she heard the sound of an email notification on her tablet. She saw who it was from and opened the message quickly.

"*Julia.*

When I typed Julia just now, I really felt like calling you Mother or Mum, but I don't know how you'd feel about that. What do you think?

You had to leave here so abruptly that we didn't say goodbye properly. I've been thinking about you constantly. I've wondered how your Peter is. I've also worried about you. Are you okay? Have you seen your specialist yet?

I hope you're not ignoring your health. You learned a lot about caring for yourself while you were here. Don't let it go to waste, please.

I'm saying this for selfish reasons. When I look at Isabel now, I see you. I want her to know you, but she's too young. You have to be around for a long time yet. Please.

When we first met, it felt like all the pieces of a puzzle had suddenly clicked into place. We are not alike in personality, but there are other things I've noticed.

I'm looking at an image on my computer screen which I just downloaded from Guy's camera. Remember when he took it? We were on that picnic at the water source where the air is moist and the grass green. We're all wearing hats and Isabel is sitting on your lap. I have my arms around the two of you. It is such a precious image, the only one I have of the three of us. I'll attach a copy to this email.

I fear that you've arrived home to chaos and you're undoing all the good we did. Find a quiet place

*and take your mind back to the house on the coast. It's
always there for you.*
> *Love*
> *Emilie x*

Julia opened the attachment and viewed the
image. Emilie and Bella's faces were full of joy. Her own
was happy, but guarded. She knew that such
happiness can be snatched away without notice.

She clicked on the reply icon and began typing.

"Emilie.

*I was very happy to receive your email. I'm
okay. Things here aren't wonderful, though. I have a
rather large list of problems now, and am having trouble
sorting them.*

To answer your questions:

*I tried to make an appointment to see the
specialist, but it hasn't happened yet.*

*Peter is in ICU and will be for some time. We
don't know the extent of the damage to his brain.*

My business is in trouble.

*There are a lot of people acting hostile and it
seems that many thought I ran off overseas with
another man.*

*You are right, I've forgotten many of the
valuable lessons I learned while with you. I must take
some time every day to practise these.*

*That beautiful photo you sent—I've made it the
background for my tablet. It will act as a reminder of
magic times.*

*In case I haven't told you, I am proud of my
beautiful daughter and her gorgeous little family. Just
remembering our time together calms me. I feel lucky
that you didn't resent me for giving you up for adoption*

because I know many people in your situation do. Your lack of judgment is part of the magic of you.
    We must spend more time together soon.
    Love
    Julia (Mum).

She re-read what she'd written. It didn't come close to conveying all the thoughts and feelings that were running through her mind, but it would do for now. She pressed send.

A thought came and it made her go to her backpack and rummage through it. Emilie had placed a box in Julia's hands at the airport, with instructions to open it when she got home. As Julia undid the ribbon and lifted the lid, she saw it was an ornament that had been created by a French glass-blower while Julia, Emilie, and Isabel had watched. Julia had loved the folds of coloured glass that glowed within a clear ball, thinking it looked like an underwater scene. She now marveled at the fact that Emilie had purchased it secretly to present to her mother later.

Julia cupped the ornament in her hands while walking from room to room. She finally settled on a space on her bedside table, where the light from the lamp would make it glow. Julia smiled when she realised that this gift would be the last thing she saw before falling asleep every night, and her first sight on waking.

CHAPTER FOUR

Julia felt blessed that Amanda was the head sister in Peter's ICU ward. Her no-nonsense approach and diplomatic handing of Peter's wife and daughters meant that Julia was able to dodge much of the stress this situation would otherwise bring.

"Hey, Julia. How are you holding up? You've got some very dark circles there!"

"Hi Amanda. It's mostly just jet lag. How's Peter? I'm meant to meet his specialist."

"Yeah, he was here just a second ago. He'll be back. Peter's condition hasn't changed. Ah, here he is!"

Introductions were made and the specialist took Julia's elbow and led her to Peter's bed. "Not good news, I'm afraid. We hoped he'd be making some signs of recovery by now, but he's much the same as when I spoke to you in Dubai."

"So what does this mean?"

"I wish I knew. It's just a waiting game at the moment."

"Nothing I should be doing?"

"You can sit with him, talk to him, and touch his hand. Bring headphones and play his favourite music. Things like that."

"Sure."

"I believe his daughters are already doing those things."

"Yes."

"I'm sorry I don't have more to tell you."

"Just one thing. Assuming he recovers to the point he can come home at some stage. What sort of nursing will he need?"

"From you?"

"Yes."

"Hard to say."

"Ballpark."

"Oh, initially I'd recommend hiring a nurse, but that would be very expensive. I think it would be a full time job, and more, for you."

"I thought it might."

"But I wouldn't be worrying about that yet."

"No, but I've got a business to run..."

"I see. Let's just cross that bridge when we come to it."

"But I have to make a decision about the business soon. This might mean I have to re-assess my involvement."

"Fair enough, but I don't have a crystal ball. This will be an unpredictable situation for a while."

"Sure...sure. I get it."

He held out his hand to shake hers. "We'll meet up again in a couple of days. Alright?"

"Okay."

As the doctor strode out of the ICU, Julia flopped down into the chair by Peter's side. Amanda came and looked at her, a slight frown between the eyes. "Well?"

"Nothing. We don't know anything."

"Yes. That about sums it up. Hey, I brought this to show you." She rummaged in a pocket and drew out a faded photograph.

Julia smiled as she saw it. "School camp!"

"You, me and Rachel."

"Raz is trying to look tough."

"Her mean look."

Julia tipped the photograph forward, trying to reduce the glare so she could see Raz's face more clearly. "I miss her, you know."

"You haven't told me what caused the falling-out."

"There wasn't one. I was just stupid. Peter here didn't like her, and back then I felt like I had to jump through hoops to please him."

"Why?"

"Because he was the big-shot lawyer. I was just the woman who ran the coffee shop in the lobby. He left his wife."

"Ah."

"Caused a lot of ill-feeling among his peers. They tried to talk him out of it."

"So, you must have been feeling insecure."

"Yes, well he wavered, you see. It took a few months for him to decide absolutely."

"So you felt you had to be better than good. Things had to be perfect."

"Yes. Everyone was giving him hell. His family, his colleagues, his friends. Even clients."

"So when he didn't like Rachel..."

"I felt I owed it to him. I slowly distanced myself from her until we argued, and then I stopped taking her calls."

"And what do you think of that decision now?"

"It was wrong. It was a shitty thing to do. I didn't even try to explain it to her."

"Why not?"

"Because I knew she'd be scornful. She doesn't pander to any man's whims, and reckons I shouldn't either."

"Yeah, well, we all make decisions under pressure that don't look right in the light of day."

"What upsets me the most is that our relationship, his and mine, didn't end up wonderful."

"Why not?"

"Oh, many reasons. Perhaps I'll buy you a drink after work one day and we'll talk."

"I'd like that. But for now, you'd better get back to your café."

Julia smiled, her face reflecting gratitude. "Thank you."

"Hello, it's Julia Hawke. I need to make an appointment to see the doctor."

"Unfortunately he is totally booked up for the next six weeks."

"I know that, but he told me to see him as soon as I got back."

"There are no appointments available—"

"For six weeks. I get that. But I think if you check with him…"

There was a sigh at the other end. "What's your number?"

Julia had to repeat it twice before the receptionist read it back correctly.

"I'll talk to Doctor when I see him next."

"When will that be?"

"When I see him next."

"Okay, I'll wait for your call."

The conversation was terminated in Julia's ear, rather rudely she felt. After a few minutes, the phone buzzed again. She hoped it was the doctor's receptionist with some news about an appointment, but when she checked the screen, she saw it was Nicholas.

"Hi Mum."

"Hi sweetie. How are the studies going?"

"Okay. Dad says I can come for dinner on Saturday night. Can we have pizza?"

"Sure. Should I pick you up?"

"Nah, I'll get there. Dad says you're to drive me home, though."

"No problems."

"See ya!"

"Bye. Love you."

As Julia exited the elevator and turned the corner, she could see the café was busy. The queue to place orders was ten deep. Julia claimed a position behind the counter, and for the next twenty minutes she smiled, scribbled orders, and fielded questions about her recent absence. Finally there was a lull.

She blew hair from her forehead and smiled at Steven and Becki. "Wow. Well done, guys."

Becki gave a weak smile in return, but Steven beamed. "We're a good team."

Julia looked around the tables and saw a solitary figure, a familiar one. It was her brother, Christopher. She grabbed two bottles of mineral water and made her way over to him.

"Hey! Great to see you!" She leaned over and

gave him a kiss.

"You too, sis. How's it all going?"

"Oh, you know."

"No, I don't."

"Peter is just the same. Mum and Dad are weird."

"Nothing new there."

"Weirder than normal. Dad wouldn't even see me the other day."

"Silly old fart."

"What are you up to?"

"Just visiting one of your lawyer friends about my case."

"Case?"

"You don't know? Oh boy."

"What are you talking about?"

"You know that deal I've been working on—the big one? Well it went bad. I owe some people big time."

"You're kidding me."

"Nope."

"Who's handling it?"

"That Damien character is the barrister. Likes you a lot"

"Oh!" Julia was silent for a moment. "Who's the instructing solicitor?"

Christopher mentioned a name that meant nothing to Julia. "I wish I could help."

"It'll sort itself out. You've got enough worries." Christopher consulted his watch. "I'm due upstairs. See you later on."

Julia watched Christopher as he moved across the lobby. He'd always considered himself a high-flyer. The fact he had no money and no backing didn't seem to deter him. It sounded like he'd come unstuck.

She had often thought that the love of a good

woman would help him. If only he could keep a relationship going for more than a few weeks.

Customers began lining up again. The café was busy for the next hour. At some point she was aware of Christopher walking back through the lobby. He stopped and began pressing on the screen of his mobile telephone. She felt her smartphone vibrate in the pocket of her apron, but wasn't able to stop to look. She waved at him.

It wasn't until much later that she remembered to check for messages. His read, "I've done something for you. I hope you don't mind. You'll find out later." Julia frowned and tucked the device back into the pocket of her apron.

She hadn't left the café in time to beat the peak hour traffic on Coronation Drive. As her car inched along the road, she watched the commuters on the City Cats with jealousy. They were gliding up the Brisbane River on almost silent catamarans.

The chatter coming from the car radio was adding to the tiredness of her stressed brain. Thinking of that made her realise the doctor's receptionist hadn't rung her back about an appointment. Julia cursed under her breath.

Finally she made the sharp turn into her street. Her house, a renovated and extended worker's cottage, was glowing in the pre-sunset light. It made the ficus trees, clipped until they resembled lollipops, look particularly green and lush.

Julia saw a flash of colour on the front step that she knew didn't belong there. She lifted her sunglasses to look more closely. A cry escaped from her throat. She braked and parked crookedly in the entrance to the driveway. Such was her excitement that she couldn't find the handle to the car door, fumbling until she had it open. She ran to the porch and looked down at the figure that was propped against the wall, sound asleep.

This was what her brother had done, brought her the one thing she really needed.

Julia stroked the green and blue hair until the woman opened her eyes.

"Raz! Oh Raz! Hello!"

PART TWO

CHAPTER FIVE

The Year 10 classroom was steaming. Rain had been falling steadily all day, and damp school girls were draped in assorted positions around desks, chairs, and the floor. The air smelled of wet wool.

Mrs. O'Brien bustled into the room. "Girls, girls! Quiet please."

Gradually the volume decreased. Mrs. O'Brien rapped the desk with a ruler. "Girls. I want you to meet our new student. Come in, Rachel."

As the new girl entered the room, twenty-three pairs of eyes looked her up and down. The girl glared back.

"Rachel has just moved here from Melbourne. I'm sure you'll make her welcome. Now let's see..." Mrs. O'Brien looked around the room. "Ah, Julia. Seeing as Amanda is away today, you can be responsible for showing Rachel around. Okay?"

Julia felt someone nudge her and snicker. It was Adrianne, the class smart arse. "Yes, Mrs.

44

O'Brien," said Julia. She was happy to make a new friend.

Rachel had attitude. Eyeliner and mascara, both banned at the school, were applied heavily. Her hair was dark and cropped short. She looked unkempt. Julia approached and gave a small smile. "Hi. I'm Julia."

"Raz."

"Raz?"

"Raz!"

"Okay, Raz. What do you want to see?"

"Dunno. What is there to see?"

"Not much!" Julia laughed. Raz looked unimpressed.

"Show me the loos."

"Sure. At least we don't have to go out in the rain for that."

Julia led the way into the corridor and along to the bathrooms. They were hideous, of course. Raz looked inside and nodded.

"Cafeteria?"

Julie crossed the corridor to the windows and pointed. "Over there. The food isn't too bad."

"Gym?"

"That big red brick building. You'll hate the PhysEd teacher. Everyone does. She's old and weird and has white foam at the corners of her mouth all the time."

"Wow."

"Where in Melbourne are you from? I went there once."

"Dandenong."

"Didn't go there. What's it like?"

Raz shrugged. "Okay."

"Were you happy to move?"

"No choice. Just had to."

"Ah, I see. Brisbane's all right."

"Rather be on the Coast."

"Gold Coast?"

"Yeah. Beaches and stuff."

A bell rang. Julia looked at her watch. "We'd better go to class. Didn't you want to...?" She nodded at the bathroom.

"Nup. Just wanted to know where they are."

"Mrs. O'Brien will take us for English now. She's good."

"Seemed okay. Hey, does everyone talk like you here?"

"How do you mean?"

"All la-de-da."

"Oh." Julia laughed. "Elocution lessons."

"Weird. Hey, I might split later."

"Split?"

"Yeah, take off."

Julia frowned. "What do you mean?"

"I don't want to be here."

"But, you've got to be!"

Raz didn't reply. She sat next to Julia during the English class, but that was the last Julia saw of her for the remainder of the day.

As the school bus approached Amanda's stop the next morning, Julia looked up from her book to find the bus shelter empty. She'd rung Amanda the night before and been told by a stressed mother that her daughter was too ill to come to the telephone. Tonsils, apparently. Julia had hoped that her friend would make an overnight recovery, to no avail.

Raz was hovering around the entrance when

Julia's bus pulled up. It didn't look like Raz had been waiting for her, but somehow Julia knew she had been. She thought she'd make the first approach.

"Hey, Rachel."

"Raz!"

"Sorry, Raz. How are you?"

The other girl shrugged. "Okay, I guess."

"Let's walk the long way up to the classrooms."

"Okay."

The 'long way' took them around the side of the property, through a small stand of trees. Raz kicked the ground and then sat down.

Julia blinked and looked down at the other girl. "C'mon, classes start soon."

"Just need to sit for a minute. Sit with me."

Julia looked at her watch and went to say something, but then just sat next to Raz and leaned against a tree.

"Don't like school, hey?"

"Nup."

"Your parents pay a lot of money to send you here."

"No, they don't."

"How come?"

"Scholarship."

"Really? Wow. You must be smart."

"Dunno."

"We had another smart girl last year. She was a bit like you. Got bored easily."

Raz didn't comment.

"Is that why you don't like school?"

"Don't like being told what to do."

"No one does. But that's just life. We're kids. Kids get told what to do."

Raz smirked, which got Julia angry. She stood

and brushed her clothes down.

"I'm going to Biology class. You can do what you want." She began walking and soon became aware that Raz was following. They took their books from the bank of lockers outside their home room and made their way to the science wing.

"Mum! Mum?"

"In the laundry."

"I've brought a friend home."

Julia's mother walked into the kitchen, wiping her hands.

"Mum, this is Rachel. Rachel, my mother."

Rachel nodded and gave a half wave. Julia's mother looked the girl up and down.

"Can she stay for a while—watch TV. Maybe have dinner?"

"If it's okay with her parents."

Raz shuffled her feet. "It's okay. Hey, have you got a colour television?" She looked excited.

"Yes, you can stay for dinner, and yes we've had colour for a long time—since it first came out. Do your homework first though."

Julia was jiggling on the spot. "Can we just walk Buster before homework?"

"Okay, but do your work straight after that."

Julia led the way to the backyard where a yawning Labrador greeted them by thumping his tail. Julia whistled and Buster rose and stretched before making his way to her. Raz hung back, watching uncertainly.

"He won't hurt you. Completely harmless. Let's go."

As they entered the street, a boy clattered down

the wooden steps of the house next door. His face broke into a smile when he saw the girls.

"Hey, Julia."

"Oh, hi!"

"Who's this?" He nodded at Raz.

"My new friend, Rachel. She likes to be called Raz."

"Raz? Cool. I'm Rob."

Julia was surprised to see that Raz had adopted a whole new pose. She had lifted her head and was looking directly into Rob's eyes. Her shoulders were straight and her chest thrust forward. She held out her hand to Rob and he shook it slowly. Julia was puzzled by this behaviour.

"We're just going for a walk."

"Have fun. Nice to meet you, Raz."

"Likewise."

The girls continued up the road, following Buster, who was on the trail of something interesting. Raz looked sideways at Julia.

"So what's Rob's story?"

"How do you mean?"

"What's he like?"

"Up himself. Has a string of girlfriends."

"Good looking. Sort of like American college boy from the magazines."

"Yeah, and he knows it."

"You're not interested?"

"Sure, but I don't feel like joining the queue."

"Do you have a boyfriend?"

"Nope. Mum reckons I'm too young. I've just turned fifteen. Do you?"

"Not at the moment."

Julia squinted at her. "How old are you?"

"Sixteen. Have been for a couple of months."

They walked in companionable silence for a few minutes. Raz kicked an aluminium can.

"I'm gonna get a job."

Julia looked at her with interest. "Where?"

"Dunno yet. I can't stand trying to get money from Mum when I need it."

"I know what you mean."

"No, I don't reckon you do, really."

"Yes, I do."

"Anyway, I'm gonna find one. Earn my own money."

"Great idea. Hey, I'm getting hungry. Want to head back for some snacks?"

"Back to your huge house with great food and colour TV? You bet."

Julia noticed her mother watching Raz over dinner, as though the girl were a puzzle that she had to solve. She asked several pointed questions, discovering that Raz's parents were divorced and that the mother had a live-in boyfriend who Raz didn't like. Her father was still in Melbourne.

It became obvious that Raz wasn't used to proper meals eaten at the dinner table. When she was served the entrée of smoked salmon, she picked up the fork intended for the main course and held it in her right hand. The salmon was then speared with the prongs, much like hay with a pitchfork, and shoved into her mouth. She had completed that course before Julia had even squeezed lemon onto her own portion. Julia had to kick her younger brother, Christopher, under the table when he began giggling at Raz's ignorance. Further questioning revealed that the girl was mostly left to her own devices at home, and had to create meals from whatever could be found in the cupboard or refrigerator. Julia had the feeling that this was never much.

After dinner, as the two girls were washing the dishes, Julia's mother came and leaned against the cupboards. She watched Julia and Raz in silence for a few minutes with her arms folded. Then she cleared her throat.

"Rachel, if you ever want to come and sleep over, or need a meal, just come by. We're usually here."

Raz looked at her through her fringe. "Thanks, Mrs. Hawke."

"You know I'm serious. Any time."

"Sure. I appreciate that."

Julia looked from Rachel to her mother in bewilderment. She'd had the distinct feeling that her mother hadn't liked Rachel on first sight and that nothing had happened to change her mind since. Why was she offering her friend food and shelter? It was weird.

From that night onward, Julia would often wake to find Raz sleeping on a mattress on the floor next to her bed, the mattress that her mother had placed there shortly after first meeting Raz. Julia felt there were things she couldn't ask about, realising that Raz's sullen curtness on these mornings was not directed at her. It was all puzzling to Julia, and it wasn't until she had some life experience of her own that she realised what terrible things the other girl might have been living through at that time.

CHAPTER SIX

Julia was stacking cups near the coffee machine in the café where she and Raz worked. It was Thursday afternoon, and their boss had just gone to the bank, clutching his bag of cash. That was the signal for the girls to slow down. Their Year 12 exams were the following week, and they took the opportunity to ask each other questions as a way of revising.

"Hey, you two!" Amanda walked in and took her usual place on the high stool near the serving area. She was jealous of Julia and Raz's jobs—her parents wouldn't allow her to take on a part-time position through her final year of schooling—so instead she just went to the café and sipped soft drinks. She was also jealous of her friends' closeness. Two years before, she had returned to school after a vicious case of tonsillitis, only to find Julia had established a tight bond with Rachel. Amanda still hung out with them, and they were careful to make sure she was never excluded, but she always felt like a hanger-on.

"Look at these!" Raz was staring out to the street as though entranced. Julia turned to see what had caught her friend's eye. There were two young men climbing from two almost identical panel vans. The men and the vans were eye-catching, but Julia wasn't sure which of these Raz was so taken with.

The vans had paintwork that made them glow. One was a light purple while the other was sea-blue. Both had roof racks that carried surfboards. There was artwork on each, fantasy images of mermaids by the sea. One showed a full-moon rising, while the other had a setting sun. Julia thought she'd never seen anything so perfect.

The two young men were on the footpath, groaning and stretching as though they'd been sitting for too long. They were of a similar age, perhaps twenty-one, and had the surfer look. They had longish hair, bleached by the elements, and were suntanned. Neither appeared to have any excess flesh, and they seemed muscular under their cut-off denims and thin t-shirts.

One was pointing to the hotel across the road. The other, who was slightly bigger in build, shook his head and looked into the café. Raz and Julia turned away quickly. The men entered and sat at a table.

"Hi!" said Raz. "Great vans. We never see them up here in Queensland—don't think they're allowed. From Victoria, are you?"

The bigger of the two had a bright smile. "Yeah. Just got here."

"Which part of Victoria? I moved up here from Dandenong a couple of years ago."

"Springvale, and he's Berwick. I'm Rick, by the way, and this is John."

"I'm Rachel, but call me Raz. This is my friend,

Julia. Oh, and Amanda is over there."

"Great. Hey, we're starving. Have you got toasted sandwiches?"

"Sure. Ham, cheese and tomato?"

"Yeah, and chocolate milk shakes. Malted. Two rounds of sandwiches each."

The girls began making up the order while the two young men murmured between themselves. Julia, hidden behind the coffee machine, was able to watch them secretly. She admired the long lashes and clear blue eyes of the slighter of the two.

As Raz passed Julia to take the sandwiches out, she gave her friend a smile and a wink. She looked mischievous.

"So," she said as she placed the food between them. "What brings you to Brisbane?"

Rick took a bite from a sandwich before replying. "On holiday, but looking to see what work opportunities there are up here. Better surfing weather."

"What do you guys do?"

"Panel beater and spray painter."

"That explains the paintwork on the vans. Great work."

"Thanks. We like them."

"Are you living in them, in the back?"

"Not yet. John here has an aunt not far from here. We're going to stay with her for a couple of weeks, then head down to the surf for a week or so."

"Where to?"

"Dunno. Kirra or Greenmount. Perhaps Snapper. We'll camp somewhere along there."

Raz gave a dramatic sigh. "Sounds dreamy."

Rick nodded at Julia. "You and your friend should tag along, don't you think, John?"

His friend nodded with enthusiasm. "Absolutely. Love to have you along."

Julia smiled to herself. *As if!* She was surprised to hear Raz's response. "Yeah, sounds great. I'd love to go. What do you say, Julia?"

"Sure." Julia said this with a note of sarcasm, but nobody seemed to notice.

"Great," said Rick, rubbing his hands together. "We'll all have a great time."

"Just give us a couple of days to sort things. We'll know for sure by early next week. Can you drop back in? Say, Tuesday?"

"Yeah. As I said, John's aunt lives not far from here, so we'll come back on Tuesday afternoon."

"And the trip will be two weeks after that?"

"What do you say, John? Leave on the Saturday?

John shrugged and nodded. "I'm easy."

"Great," said Raz. "We'll aim for that. Sounds fantastic."

Julia heard their boss returning through the back door. She whistled to Raz, who straightened her uniform and began cleaning a nearby table. "Can I get you guys anything else?"

"Some more sandwiches? We're starving!"

Julia, Rachel and Amanda were walking home slowly. The evening was soft and warm, and they didn't feel like rushing.

Julia hadn't revisited the subject of the two surfers. The whole idea was so ludicrous that she just figured Raz had played along with the men as some sort of amusement. She was surprised then, when Raz raised the subject.

"It would be great to get away with Rick and John, don't you think?"

"Sure. Impossible though."

"Nothing's impossible. We could do it."

"How?"

"I'd fix it. It wouldn't be easy, but nothing worthwhile ever is. Just imagine how good it would be, camping on the beach! The guys are really nice, too."

Amanda frowned at Raz. "You really think you could get away with going?"

"I could. Easy. It's just Jules here that we'd have to work on."

"Me? How on earth could you come up with an excuse to go away for a week? My parents aren't stupid."

"Leave it with me. You'd go, then? If I found a way?"

"It would be nice. They'd expect sex, though."

"Probably. Is that a problem?"

"Well, yes!"

"I guess you're still a virgin."

"You know I am."

"Time you lost it, I think."

"Lost what?"

"Your virginity, silly."

"Oh, I don't know. I've always had an idea of how it would happen…"

"Let me guess. You'd be in love. There would be flowers and music."

"Something like that."

"Men like girls with a bit of experience. Not too much, mind you."

"I don't know. I guess John is nice."

"And besides, you don't *have* to screw, you know. You could always say no."

"It seems implied."

"Or you could make up an excuse. Bad period. Women's problems."

"True."

"And it fits well. Our exams will be over. It won't matter if we're away for a week."

"I suppose so."

"What do you say—are you in?"

Amanda looked at them both with a frown. "You two. You're amazing. I wish I could go."

Julia was silent for a moment. "I guess so. I guess if you can find a way..."

Julia was experiencing some strange symptoms. Whenever she thought of the upcoming week away with Rick and John, she'd get stomach cramps and soaking underarms. Her mother was beginning to look at her worriedly.

"I didn't think you'd get into such as state about the exams."

Exams! That was it! A great excuse.

"Mum—it's Year 12! Of course I'm worried."

"Well, honey—take it easy. You're looking way too stressed."

"Yeah, I know. I feel bad. Stomach cramps and all that."

"It'll all be over soon, and you'll be able to take a break."

"Yeah, I should go for a holiday somewhere."

"You're not thinking of that awful Schoolies Week thing are you? I didn't think you were interested."

Julia's brain went into overdrive. She could see the sign on the noticeboard at school that had the headline "Schoolies Week!" in chunky, hand-designed lettering, with the details underneath. The dates were the same as the week the boys were heading down the coast. Whoa.

"I dunno, Mum. Could be a bit of fun and I'll need a break."

"Are Rachel and Amanda going?"

"We haven't talked about it yet."

"You wouldn't go without one of them, would you?"

"There will be others going that I'm friendly with. I'd be okay. But I'll ask Raz and Amanda. I don't even know if I'm going yet."

"Perhaps you and I should go somewhere instead. Leave Dad and Christopher behind. We could go up to the Sunshine Coast."

Julia felt something she'd never experienced before. Autonomy. Her mother was afraid Julia would go to Schoolies Week, but was powerless to prevent her. For once, Julia had the upper hand.

"Or maybe I'd go to the Gold Coast with the others but only stay a few days. I'd like to still work at the café."

"Well, I suppose that's an option. I wonder how much this would cost."

"It wouldn't cost you anything. I'd pay for it out of my own money. I've saved a lot since I started working."

Julia's mother's face crumpled for a moment. "You're growing up all of a sudden. My baby girl." She fished around the pocket of her apron and pulled out a handkerchief. "My baby girl." Now she was dabbing her eyes.

"Oh, Mum. It's not that bad. I suppose you'd feel better if Rachel or Amanda went with me. I'll give Raz a call now."

She dialed Raz's number with shaking hands and the phone seemed to ring forever until a voice said, "Hello?"

"Hey Raz. It's me. You'll never guess what!"

"What?"

"Schoolies Week." She looked around her, making sure her mother was out of earshot. "It's the same week as the boys' trip down the coast."

"I don't get it. What's Schoolies Week?"

"Don't you have it in Melbourne? It's only been going here for a few years. It's when Year 12 students go away after exams. There's a notice on the board at school about it."

"How come none of the other girls have said anything?"

"It got some bad publicity. Most wouldn't be allowed to go."

"And you are?"

"Mum doesn't want me to go, but I can use my own money. She realises she can't stop me."

Raz whistled. "Here I was, racking my brains—and you had the answer!"

Realisation came to Julia at that moment. She had just removed the obstacle that could have saved her going with the men. What had she done? Her stomach began cramping again.

CHAPTER SEVEN

Julia approached her exams in a daze. Rick and John had returned to the café, and firm arrangements had been made. Knowing she and Raz might get away with the beach camping holiday was exciting but terrifying. Her stomach cramps had lessened, but she still felt like she was treading a tightrope.

Fortunately, she had been a keen school student to that point and her exams didn't give her much cause for concern. When she asked Raz how her exams had gone, the other girl shrugged. "Failed probably. Didn't study."

Julia doubted that Raz would fail. She'd been a scholarship student for nearly three years and this covered her fees, uniform and books. Students that won those scholarships weren't likely to fail.

Amanda, not wanting to miss out on the excitement, was also trying to convince her parents it was safe for her to attend Schoolies Week. She planned on joining up with three other girls from their class, but also hoped to meet Julia and Raz at some stage through the week.

The Friday night before they went away was a time for high excitement. Raz arrived at dinnertime with several packages. The girls slipped into Julia's room and began going through the contents. Some of the items were for Julia.

Raz handed her a packet of French letters. "Just in case you let John screw you. Don't let him inside you without one of these. Under any circumstances!" She shook the packet at Julia. "Hear me?"

"Got it."

"Here's some lubricant. You might need it if things get a bit dry."

"Oh, really?"

"Yeah, you'll know if it happens."

Julia's mother called them for dinner. They shoved the incriminating objects under clothing and went to eat.

The roast chicken was a treat in celebration for the girls' departure. It was served with roast potatoes—crisp and golden—pumpkin, and peas. The gravy was delicious. Raz mopped it up with some bread while Julia's mother looked on, frowning.

When the girls had eaten until they thought they'd burst, Julia's mother cleared her throat. "Now, I know you two have your own money, but we'd like to give you both some extra cash for emergencies." She slid an envelope across the table to Julia. "Keep some each. If you don't feel comfortable in any situation, just leave. There's enough in there for a cab-ride home."

"A cab, all the way from the Gold Coast?"

"I don't expect you'll have to use it, but sometimes...well, I've seen what can go on at these events."

"Okay Mum. Thanks."

"I guess you're going to try alcohol." She sniffed. "I'd rather you didn't, but I suppose that won't stop you. Just try to stay sober. A lot of girls get into trouble after drinking too much."

Julia and Raz nodded, not daring to look at each other in case they lost control and began laughing.

"And I want telephone calls. One a day. I've put some change in the envelope for them."

"Every second day, Mum."

"Well, all right. Also, I'll drop you to the bus tomorrow, to wave goodbye."

Julia and Raz looked at each other in alarm. Julia spoke.

"Thanks Mum, but we're going to make our own way to the bus station. None of the other girls' parents are dropping them. We'd be awfully embarrassed." Her eyes were pleading, begging her mother to understand.

"Well...all right then."

"Gee, thanks Mum." Julia leapt out of her chair and rushed to give her mother a hug.

"You'll take care of Julia, won't you Raz?" Julia's father fixed the girl with a stare. She jumped. It was rare for him to even talk at the dinner table.

"Sure. No problems."

Both girls escaped from the table as soon as manners permitted. They washed and dried the dishes without fussing about the odd piece of food sticking to plates, and returned to Julia's room with mounting excitement.

After they'd finished all that had to be done, they

climbed under the covers and turned out the light. The moon was bright, and Julia could see Raz's face, white with some cream she'd spread on it.

"You've never told me—you know—how you know all these things."

"What things?"

"Men and sex. French letters and lubricant."

Raz stayed silent.

"I'm your best friend. You can tell me anything. That's what best friends are for."

Raz turned to her as though she was going to say something. Then she rolled over until she faced the other way. All Julia could see was a white shoulder, shining in the moonlight. She stayed awake for a long time, hoping her friend would turn back around and talk to her, but eventually drifted off to sleep.

CHAPTER EIGHT

The street where the girls waited was hot and noisy. From where they were standing they could see the café where they worked and tried to position themselves where their boss couldn't see them. Julia kept looking at her watch. The boys were five minutes late. Her nerves had returned with full force, and she wondered how Raz could remain so calm, while issuing last minute instructions in a low voice.

"We'll be in separate panel vans, but I'm sure that Rick and John will stay close together. If John makes you uncomfortable at all, just yell out. I'll come to you and we'll split. Okay?"

"Sure. Thanks."

"Remember, you don't have to do anything you don't want to."

"Yes, I know."

"Don't let him hurt you at all."

"I won't. What about you? Will you be all right?"

"Oh, yeah. I know how to handle myself."

They heard some musical horns and saw the two vans approaching. It looked as though the boys had washed and polished their vehicles until they sparkled. Raz squeezed Julia's arm and opened the door to Rick's van. Julia walked slowly to John's, knowing this was her last chance to back out of the whole idea. She looked through the passenger window at John and saw his brilliant smile. She gave him a grin and climbed in.

It was strange, seeing Raz in the other vehicle, talking to Rick and laughing. Raz's window was open and hair flew around her face. She had a cigarette between two fingers of her left hand. She looked wild and free—happier than Julia had ever seen her.

Julia hadn't relaxed enough to enjoy the sense of freedom, although she could feel it bubbling away under the surface. She wound her window down and smelled the fresh air. It was nice to leave Brisbane.

Rick and John played games with each other while driving. One would pull even with the other and then plant his accelerator to the floor and pull away. The other would give chase. Sometimes one would go very slowly, forcing the other to do the same.

John was in high spirits, changing music in the cassette player constantly so Julia could hear his favourite tracks. He liked The Beatles, The Rolling Stones and The Beach Boys. There was another band that Julia wasn't very familiar with—Fleetwood Mac—that he also liked. She agreed they were great.

He offered her cigarettes which she declined. Their conversation turned to television shows and movies. John was easy to talk to, and Julia enjoyed his company.

Julia didn't know the Gold Coast very well. Her parents preferred the Sunshine Coast, which was more sedate. She did realise at one point, however, that they were not far from their destination.

"We still need to get to the other end of the coast," said John. "I reckon we should get off the highway and follow the beaches." Julia saw him do something with the headlight controls. "I've just flashed Rick. We'll turn off at the next exit."

Julia felt some excitement when she finally saw The Broadwater. She smiled at John and bounced lightly in her seat. "We should stop for fish and chips," she said. "Mum and Dad always do that when we get to a beach."

"Good idea." He flashed his lights again. Rick parked where John could pull in beside him. They discussed places for fish and chips. Raz knew a shop not far away.

It was then, finally, that the sense of freedom and excitement welled up in Julia. They were away from school and parents. They were able to do whatever they wanted. She felt intoxicated.

They ate the food at a park bench overlooking the water. Seagulls flew in from all directions, squawking, looking for scraps of food. Julia threw a chip up high and watched the more nimble birds fight over the morsel.

Rick was looking around. "There's a supermarket and bottle shop down the next block. I can just make out the signs. We might stop for supplies. Perhaps you girls could get food and we'll buy drinks."

Raz nodded. "Sure. What do you want?"

"Baked beans. Lots of them. They're quick and easy and we can heat them up on a fire. Bread. Bananas. I dunno what else. You girls can decide.

What do you want to drink?"

Raz looked at Julia, who couldn't think of anything to say. What to drink? She didn't know. Her parents weren't fond of alcohol, only drinking occasionally when entertaining. Sometimes her father had a beer. "Southern Comfort," said Raz. We'll both have that. She reached into her pocket for money, but Rick waved it away.

The supermarket was small, but the girls found all they wanted. They added more to the trolley than the boys had asked for. Tea and coffee. Soft drinks. They split the bill between them and went back to the vans to unload. The boys had two cartons of drinks including beer, Southern Comfort and several bottles of Asti Spumante. "Leg opener," said Raz in an undertone. Julia didn't understand what she meant.

When everything was stowed, Rick rubbed his hands together. "Excellent. Let's find a good camping spot near Currumbin."

The boys' equipment was basic, verging on non-existent. They hadn't told the girls they needed any cutlery or plates, so when it came to eating, they ended up doing it in two shifts—Raz and Rick first. Nobody minded on the first night, because they were still fairly satisfied by the fish and chips. They spoke lazily about finding some more equipment the next day.

The boys had parked the vans with the rear hatches opening onto the beach. They had unpacked a cool box and poured ice over a bottle of Spumante. A fire was started and baked beans heated. When it came to her turn, Julia spooned some baked beans onto a piece of bread and rolled it up like a sausage. Raz laughed at her and Julia kicked Raz's foot.

The beer was produced and the Southern Comfort opened. Julia didn't want any at that time, but thought she would have some later. Raz sloshed some into a tin cup and took a mouthful. She coughed. The second mouthful went down easier.

As the sky darkened, the four began swapping stories about their lives. Julia was astonished at the boys' lack of interest in anything remotely cultural. They didn't read. They had left school early to commence their apprenticeships and seemed to have spent their life since then in pubs and nightclubs. Their knowledge of world events was limited. It was only when they spoke about surfing that Julia could sense a quality of something deeper. Their relationship with nature and the beauty of the ocean seemed to create a place in their souls from which poetry flowed. Rick and John wouldn't have called it poetry, however. It was just two blokes talking about the surf.

They had met as first-year apprentices, both hired by a gruff panel-beater in Chadstone. Their weekends were free to chase waves or work on their vans, and they seemed inseparable. Julia, having just read a novel about World War Two, had a flash of insight. She knew that if these two young men ever went to war, they'd do so together, supporting each other through whatever trials befell them.

The moon rose out of the water, past full but resplendent nonetheless. Its red face gave way to orange and then yellow. Finally it became silver and shone onto the sand, turning it white.

Rick popped the plastic cork from the bottle of Asti Spumante. Wine, in the form of foam, spewed from the top, causing him to jump back in alarm. He sloshed equal parts into metal cups and passed them around. "To our holiday on the beach!"

John, Raz and Julia echoed his toast and downed the bubbling wine. Julia wrinkled her nose, finding the drink too sweet. Rick poured more into her cup with a smile. Raz was frowning. "Careful, Jules. This stuff can take you by surprise."

Rick laughed. "Nah. Like lemonade. Drink up."

Julia thought back to Raz's puzzling comment when the wine was being loaded into the panel van. Leg opener. Of course. She smiled and winked at Raz.

John produced a guitar from his van and began singing folk songs. His voice was reedy, but he could hold a tune. When he hit a high note, it echoed around the headland.

A breeze blew up the beach, and Julia shivered. She remembered seeing a blanket in the back of John's van and fetched it. The whole rear of the van was taken up with a foam mattress and pillows. It looked inviting. Julia yawned as she walked back to the others around the fire.

Raz was leaning against Rick, who was stroking her bare arm. Julia thought that looked nice so moved closer to John and snuggled into his side. He put an arm around her. She felt happy. The waves were gentle now, rolling in with a soft rhythm that made her sleepier.

John stood. "Let's hit the sack. I want to be out there first up in the morning." He nodded toward the dark expanse of water, lit only by the moon, now high in the sky.

"Sure." Rick rose and held out his hand to Raz. He pulled her to her feet and led her to the back of his van. They both crawled inside.

Julia yawned again and realised she'd have to empty her bladder before falling asleep. There were no toilets. She took a tissue out of her bag and walked into the bush, trying to find a private place. She crouched down, but heard something scrambling around in the undergrowth. An animal? Julia moved again and was finally able to relieve herself.

John was sitting on the edge of the mattress, brushing his feet. "Trying not to get sand in the bedding." Julia nodded. She removed her sandals and rubbed the soles of her feet together. Then she brushed them with her hands. She lay on top of the bedding and smiled at John. "It's been a great day. Goodnight!"

Julia lay facing the side of the van. She felt John slide in next to her. He lay with his arm around her waist and wriggled in close. She ignored him. Time went by, and it was only when she heard his breathing change into a gentle snore that she allowed herself to fall asleep.

The sun rose in almost the same place the moon had on the previous night. There was nothing to protect against the light, so Julia was awake early, groggy and shielding her eyes against the brightness.

John was lying on his stomach, still sleeping. Julia watched him for a few minutes, marveling at his firm chin and flawless skin. Not a blemish in sight, but there were hairs sprouting around his jawline. She liked his face, which was open and friendly. It appeared guileless. She felt as though she could become very fond of him. Maybe he could be her first boyfriend. The thought made her happy.

Julia smelled something unpleasant and realised it came from the bedding. It was a stale odour of unwashed fabrics, made worse by the rising temperature of the van. She thought she could even detect traces of cheap perfume. The pillow case, once white, was soiled.

She had been puzzled initially by Rick and John. They were travelling together and could easily have shared one vehicle to save fuel costs. Why two vans? Now she understood. It was so they could pick up girls, like her and Raz. This thought disturbed her until her customary optimism kicked-in. Once John had a serious girlfriend all that would stop, and that girlfriend could be her. If the boys found jobs in Brisbane, that was.

She felt a pain in her lower abdomen, and wondered about it, knowing that her period wasn't due for another two weeks. She slid out of the van and crouched in the bushes. She passed wind and the pain went away. Giggling, she ran down to the water's edge.

There wasn't a person or animal in sight. Nor were there any clouds. It was a perfect day. The slightest of breezes blew up the beach. She was warm and happy.

Knowing she'd gone to bed with her makeup on, she tried to rectify that with sea water. The mascara came off fairly easily and she otherwise just splashed her face. Her knickers felt dirty and she was sure they'd smell. She had clean pairs, but didn't want smelly ones in her bag. Tugging them down her legs, she let them fall into the water and swirled them around with her foot. This was made harder by the flow of the waves.

All that remained covering her was a skirt, blouse and bra. She looked behind her to the vans, checking that the others were still asleep, before removing these and tossing them onto the sand, out of reach of the waves. She plunged under the surface, gasping as the cold hit her midriff. A decent-sized wave was rolling in and she dived under it. Exhilarated, she broke the surface on the other side of the wave with a whoop of excitement.

Figuring that the boys would wake soon, she left the surf reluctantly and held her sandy clothes across her body. She hadn't thought of a towel. Frowning, she moved until she was at the front of the vehicles, where the others couldn't see her. She felt a pain in her lower abdomen again, but ignored it. She knew it was wind.

Minutes went by and her body had dried enough to put her clothing back on. She tried combing her hair with fingers, but they stuck in tangles. She crouched in front of a side mirror on John's van to check the mascara had come off cleanly.

She was thirsty. Why hadn't they thought to buy water? She looked left and right and then began walking north, hoping for a park which should have a tap. She walked for fifteen minutes, then turned back. Now she was even thirstier.

When Julia returned to the vans, she saw Rick and John maneuvering themselves into wetsuits. Their surf-boards were already unloaded from the roof-racks and taken from their protective covers.

As Julia approached, they turned and greeted her. Rick grabbed his board and ran into the surf. John smiled and asked if she slept well. She nodded and asked if they had any water. John shrugged and ran after Rick, calling back to say they'd have a quick surf before breakfast and that maybe she could set up the fire?

Set up the fire? She tried to remember how John had done it the previous afternoon. He'd placed small twigs and branches over the circle of rocks. Larger pieces of wood went over those. Did he use paper? Where were the matches?

Raz was stirring in the back of Rick's van. Julia went and gave her a shake. "C'mon sleepyhead. We're in charge of lighting a fire." Raz mumbled and slid feet first from the van, pushing herself along with her arms.

"I guess it's baked beans for breakfast." Julia looked at the tins of food forlornly.

"Guess so."

Raz had a small flicker of flame working on the fire. She blew gently until it caught onto the dry wood. Julia opened the beans and stood them next to the fire. Raz picked up the jar of instant coffee. "How about tea and coffee? The boys have a billy somewhere, don't they?"

"Yes, but no water."

"What are we meant to drink?"

"Don't know. But I have a thirst I can't jump over."

Raz situated the beans closer to the fire. She pushed some bread onto a forked tree branch and held it close to the flames. The air was filled with the smell of toast. Julia became ravenous.

By the time the boys emerged from the surf, laughing and shaking the water from their bodies like dogs, the girls had eaten toast and beans. Rick and John ate quickly, talking about how good the surf was. They were keen to return to the waves.

"We need water," said Julia. "I'm really thirsty."

"Have beer. That's what we're doing." Rick demonstrated this by taking a can from the cool box and lifting the ring-pull. He handed it to John before getting one for himself.

"No, I need water."

"Should have bought some yesterday."

"I didn't know we'd be somewhere without taps."

"Okay. After our next surf we can go for a drive." John said this with a tone of annoyance.

"How long will that be?"

"A while. The surf's too good to leave. Have a beer."

Julia wrinkled her nose and had a mouthful from John's can. She washed it around her mouth and spat it out. She found her bag in the van and spent a few moments organising her belongings. She took out a book and began reading it under a tree, which had no hope of shading her from the morning sun.

The boys went back into the surf. Time ticked by slowly. Julia felt a headache coming on. Raz was doing sketches of the scene before them, drawing the horizon first with a steady hand and then filling in details. Occasionally they heard one of the boys whoop with delight as they caught a good wave. Raz would smile, but Julia was scowling.

It was close to midday before the boys emerged from the surf again. They were glowing with excitement and good health. Rick stopped in front of the fire and looked down. "Didn't you girls keep the fire going? How are we going to warm up the baked beans for lunch?"

"We'll get some other food when we go to buy water." Julia said this firmly. "I'm sick of baked beans."

Rick laughed. "Listen to the princess here. 'I want water! I don't want baked beans!'" He said this in a high voice, mimicking hers. "We'll have to call you Princess Polly." He turned to Raz. "Won't we!"

"Hey, Julia's my best friend. Don't ask me to pick on her. She's just been brought up in a wealthy family. She's not used to roughing it. Leave her alone." Raz was glaring at Rick, and he dropped his gaze.

"Okay. No need to get your knickers in a knot. John, you go, will you? I don't want anybody else to get our camping spot. Bring us back some fish and chips."

"Yeah, no problems. Come on then, Julia."

There was a service station a few kilometres

from where they were camped. There were no fish and chip shops. The service station didn't sell food to go— just assorted items in packets and tins. John collected some more baked beans while Julia stocked up on water. She found paper plates and plastic cutlery, but couldn't see anything other than the beans that could be heated in its can by the fire. John grabbed two more bags of ice. Another pain hit Julia in the abdomen and she winced. John paid for the food as she ran for the toilets. There was only wind, nothing else.

When John and Julia returned, Rick and Rachel were in the shallows. Rachel was on a surfboard and Rick was showing her some surfing moves. John started the fire, and the baked beans were warmed up. Everybody ate quickly. Rick went back to teaching Rachel, while John applied some wax to his board. When they thought their lunch had digested enough, the boys ran back into the water.

Pains hit Julia in the stomach again. She tried to ignore them by reading her book but they were getting worse. Raz asked if she was all right.

"No, I'm not! I don't think I can stand a whole week of this! Baked beans that give me wind. Boredom. No toilets. No running water. It's horrid!"

Raz laughed. "It's not that bad. Give it another day or so. You might get to enjoy it. Besides, I think John likes you."

"I like him too. I'd just rather we were more comfortable."

That night, when offered Asti Spumante, Julia downed several cups. When they went to bed, she turned her back on John and fell into a deep sleep. When she woke in the morning, hung-over and with pains, she found John pressed in to her back, his hardness evident against her buttocks. She heard him sliding his jocks off, and then he began to lift her skirt. She said, 'No!" and moved away.

He followed her. "Don't be such a tease. I need you. Feel this!" He grabbed her hand and pushed himself against it.

"Stop it. That's disgusting."

"It's not disgusting. Why do you think we brought you girls here? You must've known."

He reached around and began touching her between the legs. "No! I said no!" She tried to move further from him, but found herself jammed against the side of the van. She began sliding down to the foot of the bed.

"Oh, no you don't." He grabbed her under the armpits and slid her upwards, seemingly without effort. "You can't play the princess with me. You knew what you were here for." He slid himself between her thighs. She could feel him at the entrance to her vagina. She moved to scream, but he clamped his hand across her mouth. He spit into his other hand and rubbed the moisture onto himself. Then he began forcing his way inside her.

She tried to bite his hand, the one holding her mouth. When that didn't work, she began bucking and kicking, but he was relentless. He seemed too big, and he was entering her too fast. She could feel flesh tearing. "A wet check!" she tried to say. She said it again.

He realised what she meant. "Don't need it. Had bad mumps last year. Doc says I'm probably sterile. I'll pull out when I come, just in case."

She still kept bucking and kicking. She heard him groan and shudder, felt the wetness. He slumped against her, like a rag doll.

Julia lay shocked and dazed for a moment. She

couldn't think straight—couldn't form ideas. John began snoring and this galvanised her into action. She slid quietly out of the van and ran down to the water's edge, wincing as the salt hit her inflamed flesh. As she washed all traces of him away, she saw blood staining the other fluids. The sight of this reminded her that she had now lost her virginity in probably the worst way possible. Previously she'd been upset and hurt. Now she was angry.

Moving to the van, she reached for her bag and put it across her shoulder. She saw the keys to the van in the ignition. She looked in the other van, and saw the keys in that one as well. She removed both sets and flung them into the bushes.

Raz's bag was lying in the sand. Julia picked it up and hoisted it on to the other shoulder. She pulled on her friend's foot. "Psst. Psst. Come on. We're going."

"What?"

"Now. Come on. Before the guys wake up."

"Jeez, Jules. I thought you were going to give it a bit longer—"

"I'm going. You can stay if you want." She threw Raz's bag back into the sand and began walking. She heard Raz running up behind her.

"Okay, we'll go. What's your plan?"

"Haven't got one. We're leaving. That's the plan."

Raz looked at her narrowly. "Nothing wrong, is there?"

"No."

"I need to pee."

"Wait. There's a service station up the road."

They heard a car approaching. It drew even with them. A police car.

"Let me guess. Schoolies?"

Raz turned and looked at the officer. "Yeah. Some guys dumped us. Can you take us to Surfers?"

"Sure. Jump in."

Raz leaned over toward Julia. "What's the name of the hotel where Amanda is?"

"Can't remember. It's the one we told Mum we were staying at." At the thought of her mother, Julia felt tears welling in her eyes.

"I remember." Raz told the officer the name of the hotel.

They were silent for the rest of the journey. The officer looked at Julia in the rear-vision mirror a few times, but didn't make comment. It wasn't until they had reached the hotel that he asked if she was all right. She just nodded, dumbly.

She thought about telling the officer what happened. He seemed nice enough, but how stupid did the story sound? She'd lied to her parents and gone off with some surfer guys. She'd slept in the back of the van with one of the men. She was asking for trouble and she got it. Stupid, stupid, stupid. She'd heard about rape cases in court and how bad they could be for the girl—reckoned she'd be laughed at.

The hotel was basic, but clean-looking. Both Julia and Raz's names were in the booking, so the receptionist handed them keys without a murmur. They opened the door to their room quietly, in case Amanda was still asleep. The room was dark and the bed unmade, but there was no sign of their friend.

Julia threw her bag onto the other bed and looked around her as if she'd misplaced something. After a moment she lowered herself onto the bed and lay on her side, tucking her legs up to her chest.

Raz opened the curtains. "Wow! Nice view. The water looks great. We could go for a swim."

"No. I just want to lie here for a minute. Then I'm going to have a shower and get changed."

The door to the room burst open. Amanda bounced in with an exclamation of delight. "Raz! Jules! It's so good to see you! How come you're back so early?"

Julia remained silent. Raz shrugged. "Wasn't much fun. Julia hated it."

"You two can have a better time here. Trouble is, the others just get drunk all the time. Adrianne was vomiting in the gutter last night. Silly bitch. I had to hold her hair back."

"I'm going home." Julia's voice sounded thin and weak. The wind pains were back again and she curled into a ball.

Amanda frowned. "Are you okay?"

"They fed her too many baked beans," said Raz. "She's feeling sick. Stomach pains."

"Baked beans? Like from a tin?"

"Yep. Breakfast, lunch and dinner. Jules wasn't used to them."

Amanda shuddered. "Ugh. Can't say I blame her. How horrible." She was rewarded with a weak smile from Julia. "We can get some decent food for you here, though. No need to go home yet. Stay and have some fun."

Julia couldn't even think of the right words to say to her friends. She was experiencing feelings she'd never had before, feelings of inadequacy. She felt naïve and stupid, too young and protected to be out in the larger world. Attending an all-girls school meant she hadn't dealt with the opposite sex on any regular basis, except for her father and younger brother. She didn't know what made boys and men tick—had no understanding of their urges and impulses. She had been out of her depth. All she wanted to do at that moment was return home where she felt safe. Even the thought of walking through the front door of her house made her feel better.

She sat up and pulled her bag towards her. "I'm going home. Straight after a shower."

Amanda's face lost its happy glow. "Oh. I thought the three of us could have such fun. Will you stay, Raz?"

The other girl shook her head. "Nah. I'll go with Julia. We might be able to pick up some more work at the café. There's a movie Jules and I want to see, too."

Julia smiled at her friend. There was no such movie. She knew Raz was probably longing to stay on the Gold Coast and have fun, but wouldn't do so without Julia. They'd catch the bus together and travel back to Brisbane. Raz would make sure she got home safely. Then they would hang out together for the rest of the week. Just the two of them. Just how they liked it.

CHAPTER NINE

Julia opened the gate and was greeted by Buster's wolfish grin and wagging tail. She spent a few minutes patting him and then went through the front door.

"I'm home!"

Her mother looked around the kitchen doorway. "Back already! I was wondering what time you'd call today. Come through. I'm just making a cake."

"Is it a chocolate cake? Yum!"

"How was it?"

"Okay. Not marvellous. Got bored."

Julia's mother looked up from the cake and gave her a searching look. "Did the others come back with you?"

"Just Rachel. She's gone to the café to see if we can get some work this week."

"Oh, that reminds me. Your boss from the café rang."

"What did he want?"

"He's got trouble with staff. Hoped you and

Rachel could work some extra shifts if you came back early. Said he'd pay you a bonus."

"Great. Raz will sort it with him then. I'll go and unpack."

"So everything was all right? Nothing bad happened, did it?"

"Of course not, Mum. I just didn't enjoy it there. I'll tell you all about it at dinner time. Raz can tell you stories too. I'm a bit tired. I'll go and lie down for a while."

The effort of appearing normal to her astute mother had drained her. She threw herself face-down on her bed and began crying.

With school behind them, the girls could work long hours and earn extra money. Julia did her best to erase the memory of John from her mind. She decided that there was nothing she could do about it now, and it was best forgotten. Chalk it up to experience.

Raz, in her usual form, began plotting a new adventure. She first raised the idea during a quiet time at work. The café was warm, and the girls had pushed back sections of the folding doors until the footpath had become part of the premises. There was one woman with a toddler and she was feeding him cookies while reading a magazine. She was in the far corner of the café, out of earshot.

Raz stopped wiping down a machine and looked at Julia. "We should take a gap year."

"A what?"

"You know. A year off before university."

"I'm not sure I'm going to Uni"

"Really? I assumed you were. You said you wanted to do an Arts degree."

"Only for something to do. Suddenly that seems boring. I haven't done anything about it at all. Mum keeps asking."

"Yeah, I'm the same. That's why I'm saying we should take a gap year."

"And do what?"

"Go overseas."

"Wow, really? Gee, I don't know if I'm ready for that."

"Yeah. Absolutely. Of course you're ready."

"Where?"

"Dunno. Europe…" She held her arms wide and began turning in tight circles. "England, South America, India…"

Julia blew out her cheeks. Her own parents had only travelled as far as New Zealand. "When?"

"Depends. If we save as much money as we can—maybe even get second jobs—I reckon we'd have enough to leave in July."

"Wouldn't it cost an awful lot?"

"I reckon your Mum and Dad would give you some."

"What about you?"

"I'll have enough. You can travel really cheaply if you don't mind putting up with a little discomfort."

"I suppose so. Would we fly?"

"Dunno. Need to look at all the options. I heard you can get cheap berths on merchant ships." She looked over Julia's shoulder and smiled. "Look, it's the guys."

Julia could tell that her face had drained of blood. "Oh, no!"

"What?"

"I don't want to see him."

"John? Duck out the back. I'll talk to them."

Julia went out the back door and waited for what seemed like an eternity. She was having trouble controlling her breathing.

"All clear." Raz was standing at the back door, wiping her hands on a cloth. "What was all that about? Why didn't you want to see John? And they had some story that you took their car keys. They seemed really pissed off."

"I didn't take their damned keys anywhere. They're just crazy, uncouth louts. I hate them!"

"Anyway, they're leaving for Melbourne today— going home. That's the last we'll see of them. Shame. I really liked Rick. " She looked at Julia with a frown. "One day you'll tell me what really happened with John."

Raz found them second jobs, packing shelves in a major supermarket at night. Life was busy for the two girls. Neither had boyfriends and didn't think much about that. It wasn't through lack of opportunity—there were many men, young and old, who would hang around the café in the hopes of catching the girls' eyes—but Julia ignored them and Raz followed her example.

On nights off they went to movies or hung out at Julia's place. They never went to Raz's house. Julia had realised early in their friendship that it was a place that nobody wanted her to visit, not Raz nor Julia's parents.

After they'd been packing shelves for a few weeks and saving as much money as they could, Julia began to tire easily. She felt sick, exhausted and limp. "I think I've been working too much."

"Nonsense. You're young and healthy. Tell me

your symptoms."

"Weak, tired. Not hungry. Food makes me feel sick. I even threw up yesterday morning."

Raz frowned. "When was your last period?"

"Um, not sure. Haven't had one in a while. Just before we went to the Gold Coast. I'm never regular, though."

"You and John. You screwed?"

"Sort of."

"Did you *sort of* use a wet check?"

"Didn't need to. John said he couldn't father a baby. He'd had mumps."

"Jesus, Jules! What did I tell you! Make sure you use the wet checks no matter what!"

"He said he'd pull out, before he…you know… just in case. You think I'm pregnant? "

"I bet you are."

Julia closed her eyes. Could it be? Is that what was wrong with her? She'd been imagining terrible diseases. But surely not. Surely fate wouldn't allow it after what happened. She didn't deserve that. It would be so unfair. No, surely not.

The supermarket night fill supervisor was walking down the aisle. The two girls started filling shelves quickly. Raz's actions suggested anger. "I guess that's the end of our holiday plans."

"Oh, I didn't think of that. I suppose so. It could just be a sickness, though."

"What will you do, if it is a baby?"

Julia shook her head. "I don't know. What do you think?"

"I think you should make an appointment to see a doctor. Make sure he isn't one you know, and use a fake name. The appointment should be at a time when we're both not working so I can come as well."

"Oh, alright."

"Ask what they need you to take for a pregnancy test. You might have to pee in a bottle."

"What? Really?"

"Yeah. Do all that as quickly as you can. Let me know when."

The waiting area of the doctor's surgery was full. There were wailing babies and untidy mothers. There were men studying newspapers.

Julia went to the reception desk. The woman was frowning at her. "Yes?"

"I have an appointment. I'm very early. It's with Doctor Wilson." She slid the urine sample across the counter. "Here."

"What are we doing with that?"

Julia leaned forward. "Testing, for a baby."

The receptionist looked at Julia's fingers that were splayed across the counter. Julia flushed. She should have thought of that. A ring. Raz would have made sure she had one. She began feeling a sense of dread, realising that coming without Raz may not have been the best idea.

"I see." The woman's voice was terse. "And your name is?"

"Um, Cathy. Cathy Smith."

"Take a seat, *Miss* Smith. Doctor will see you in a while."

Was everybody in the waiting room looking at her? It seemed so as she scanned the room for a spare seat. There was one beside a large woman, but she had her packages on it. Julia went to the wall and leaned against it. A door opened and a man called, "Mrs. Hodge?" The large woman stood and grabbed her possessions. Julia plopped down in one of the now-vacant seats. Her heart was beating quickly.

One of the men had body odour and it made Julia feel like she was going to vomit. She picked up a magazine and began fanning herself with it until she felt better. She opened the first page and realised it was a publication for new mothers. She shut the cover and put the magazine down.

There was a novel in her bag that she opened to the bookmarked page. Time went by, and she began to feel sleepy. Names were called. She became aware of somebody standing before her, talking. "Miss Smith? You are Miss Smith, are you?"

Julia stood and the room began to sway. She clutched the man's arm. "Sorry. Yes. That's me."

"Are you all right?"

"Yes, I'm fine now." She took her hand away.

"Come this way."

The doctor sat behind a desk. It was large and made of dark wood. It seemed too big for the room. "Now, Miss Smith. I understand you have come for a pregnancy test."

"Yes."

"When did you last menstruate?"

Julia gave him the date.

"And you have had intercourse since then?"

"Yes." Julia's voice was small.

"I see." He stood and walked to the rear of the room where there was a bed and a curtain. He pulled at the curtain until it hid the bed. "Go in and take your skirt off. You can leave your undergarments on. Cover yourself with the sheet."

Julia did as she was told. "I'm ready!"

The doctor began palpitating her lower abdomen. "Yes, about ten weeks. You can get dressed now."

When Julia re-emerged, the doctor was behind his desk, scribbling on a card. He gave her a hard look.

"Didn't they give you sex education at school?"

"Um, no."

"Private Girls College then?"

"Yes."

The doctor sighed. "Silly girl. I see so many, just like you. Not an ounce of common sense."

Julia felt the flush rising. It prickled her scalp. The feeling of dread was increasing. Why hadn't she brought Raz? Why pick this day to decide to be a bit independent? Stupid.

The doctor continued. "And that Schoolies Week. I expect to see a lot more girls like you in the near future. So what are you going to do?"

"I don't know." The tears were welling. She swallowed hard.

The doctor continued scribbling. "Stay away from abortionists. Many are unqualified and you could end up with an infection that could take your life."

"Oh..."

"Tell Maria, that's the receptionist, to give you some pamphlets. Homes for unmarried mothers. Best get your name down at one of those quickly. There is usually a waiting list."

The doctor stood abruptly and waved Julia toward the door. She rose, unsteadily, and moved through to the reception desk. The doctor handed the card to the woman and she gave him another. "Mr. Johnston?" The two men disappeared into the surgery.

Julia approached Maria again. The receptionist was reading the card with raised brows. "So, we need some pamphlets on homes, do we *Miss* Smith?"

Julia felt a cry catch in her throat. She turned

and fled through the main doors. As she descended the steps into the street she felt something rising in her—overwhelming her—and could now name it. Shame. She felt dirty and unworthy. For the first time in her life she felt inferior to those around her.

This shame, caused by the doctor and his receptionist, who both lacked any trace of compassion or empathy, would stay with her for many years. It would cause her to lock away this part of her, the part that held the shameful secret, where nobody could reach it. She would hold this back from her parents, friends, lovers, husbands, and children. It would cause damage to every relationship in her life. Except the one with Raz.

"Jeez, Jules. You should have taken me with you." Raz had her arm around her sobbing friend, trying to console her.

"I know! I was stupid. I needed you there. They were so rude!"

"Yeah. Dickheads."

"The doctor reckons I should go into a home for unmarried mothers."

"What do you want to do?"

"Not that."

"Abortion?"

"Ugh. Seedy. And the doctor says it's dangerous."

"You could always tell your Mum. It would come as a shock, but she might be able to help."

"I couldn't stand the hysteria. Their only daughter. Just imagine what Dad would say!" Julia shuddered.

Raz began counting on her fingers. She

stopped and nodded. "How about this—we still keep working hard—it won't do you any harm, and leave for overseas before you start showing much. You could wear a girdle or something to hide the baby until we're ready. We still go overseas, and when you have the baby, leave it at an orphanage. Somewhere Catholic like Italy where this sort of thing is common."

Julia wiped her eyes and looked at Raz with a hopeful expression. "Golly! Do you reckon it would work?"

"Yup."

"You'd have to look after me when I was really pregnant. Mightn't be much fun."

"We'll make up for it after you have the baby."

"You'd really do this for me?"

"Hey, don't forget I got you into this. Seems only right. What about John? He's responsible. We could hit him up for money. We know he works at a panel-beaters in Chadstone. Shouldn't be too hard to find."

Julia shook her head vehemently. "Complicate things too much. Besides, I don't want to see those guys ever again."

Although Julia had gone along with the idea of taking a gap year and going overseas, she'd been experiencing doubts about her capacity to be independent, given her handling of the situation with John. Her pregnancy had now over-ridden any concerns. She had to go.

CHAPTER TEN

"It seems silly to me," said Julia's mother, who was clearly unhappy on that cold winter's morning, "that you have to fly all that way south to catch a flight that passes over Brisbane again hours later."

The airport was almost deserted, the shops still closed. The first leg was a domestic flight to Sydney, where they would transit for two and a half hours before departing to London via Hong Kong.

"It was the cheapest fare, Mum. We don't mind."

"You might after you've been travelling all that time. I guess you're young, though." This was said with a sigh.

Christopher was standing apart from the group, leaning against one of the huge windows, an arm resting across the glass. He was focused on the activity taking place on the tarmac.

"No one seeing you off then, Rachel?" Julia's mother was looking at the girl with concern.

"Bit early for my mother."

"Oh, I see."

Some doors opened, and people wearing airline uniforms began preparing for boarding. A line formed which consisted mostly of men carrying briefcases.

Julia smiled at her mother. "We'd better get in line. Christopher! Come and say goodbye!"

Her brother came running and gave her a dry kiss on the cheek. Moving to Rachel, he gave her the same, after which he returned to gaze out of the window.

Julia walked over to her father and kissed him goodbye. She felt him slide something into her pocket, then saw him give her a slow wink. She winked back.

Julia's mother was opening her arms wide and had tears in her eyes. "Come and give your Mum a big hug."

Julia nearly broke then—nearly allowed herself to disappear into that maternal embrace, against the familiar ample bosom of her mother. She nearly blurted out about the baby, knowing that her mother would eventually allow practicalities to overrule anger and disappointment. Her mother could fix things. That was her art.

But instead, Julia walked into that embrace, only allowing her mother an arms-length hug, scared that the hard bulge of her growing uterus could be detected despite the girdle. The embrace was light and swift.

Her mother's whole face began to tremble. "Too grown up for a proper hug now then, are we?"

Julia's father was watching this interaction with a frown. He moved over to his wife and placed his arm around her in a rare gesture of support.

And it was this—the arms-length embrace with

her mother—that haunted Julia for the whole of her and Raz's trip. What if something happened to her mother? What if she got sick and died or had an accident while Julia was away? Would their last physical contact be that quick, cold clutch?

Or maybe it would be Julia who met with an untimely death. The childbirth gone wrong, or an unsafe bus in a poor country. Anything could happen.

These thoughts were running through Julia's mind as the aircraft gathered speed. Tears were running down her face. Raz nudged her. "Hey, everything is great. Don't worry. What did your Dad give you? I saw him slip something into your pocket."

Julia produced an envelope. Inside was one thousand dollars in cash and a credit card in her name. There was a note which read, "Princess. A bit extra spending money. The credit card is for emergencies only. I love you. Come home safely."

Julia's father, a man not given to demonstrations of affection, had outdone himself. Julia began sobbing all over again.

There were numerous delays in Hong Kong which resulted in a late arrival into London. Raz's cousin, an actor, was waiting for them in the baggage claim area, holding a sign that bore Rachel's name and an Australian flag. He transported the two girls to his digs in Earl's Court; where many Australians had created their own community.

After a week of attending plays and dining out, Julia and Raz boarded a ferry destined for France. Half an hour into this voyage, Julia visited the bathroom and wriggled out of her girdle. She stuffed it into the rubbish chute with a sigh of relief.

They moved aimlessly around Europe for several weeks, visiting Spain and Italy. Finally they arrived back in France close to the time when Julia's baby was due to make its entrance into the world.

CHAPTER ELEVEN

The girls sat in silence, appreciating the view of the French valley. Grape vines stretched as far as the eye could see, interrupted only by tiny villages and chateaux that were straight from the pages of fairy tale books. Tiny birds darted in and out of the greenery

"Word is that the harvest will start early this year." Raz flopped down onto the seat beside Julia and tore at a baguette with her teeth. "I could probably start work in a week or so."

"There must be something I can do as well."

"I don't think so. The rules are that you have to be very physically fit."

"So, do you have to apply?"

"Yeah, there's a sign-on day coming up at the big winery where the chateau is. I'll go and put my name down. It's on Tuesday."

"You could ask if there's any other work."

"Darling, you look like you're just about to split open. No one will employ you!"

"I've still got a few weeks to go. So, how long does the harvest last?"

"Dunno. Maybe one to three weeks, depending on weather, but it seems like the sun will be shining. If there's no rain then the time will be shorter."

"Are you paid for rainy days if there are any?"

"Nope. Only the days you pick."

"That's a shame."

"It's okay. We've still got cash."

"What will we do after that?"

Raz sloshed some wine into her glass and lit a cigarette. "Olive picking further down south, but I think we'll stop here and wait until you have the baby first."

Julia looked down at her backpack wearily. "So, is there anywhere to stay here?"

"The guy behind the bar said to try a place just up the road a bit. If I get a job on the grapes, accommodation and food will be provided."

"For you, maybe."

"Yeah, I know.

"I'll still come with you for sign-on. You never know."

The line of applicants for the job of harvesting grapes ran halfway up the driveway which led to the barn. This was a separate driveway to the decorative, tree-lined road that led to the chateau. This one was dry and dusty, and the pickers were getting hot and restless.

There was a stir as the barn door opened. A middle-aged man dressed in brown working garb stared at the applicants and then began propping the doors open. He disappeared into the interior again, and when he re-emerged he had a folding table which he proceeded to assemble. A chair was added, a manila folder placed on the table, and he sat down.

He waved to the first person and then made a rapid motion which meant, hurry up. The young man ran up to the desk and began talking. The foreman shook his head and waved him away.

This happened to the first three people. Julia noted how Raz watched carefully, trying to establish the rules so she wouldn't be one who was rejected.

They had been standing in the sun for over half an hour. Julia rubbed her back. "I think I'm going to sit in the shade over there—under the tree. I'll join you when it's nearly your turn."

Raz nodded. Julia propped herself against the tree and watched the goings on at the table. The fourth applicant showed the foreman his passport and a piece of paper. The foreman nodded and gave him a form. Julia saw Raz reach into her backpack for the travel documents.

Julia had been so intent on those goings on that she didn't notice a man approaching until his voice came from beside her. "It is hot, non?"

"Yes, er, oui."

"Where are you from?"

Julia looked up at the man. He was casually, but impeccably, dressed. He wore camel trousers and navy shirt, and had a yellow jumper draped over his shoulders. His shoes had a high shine, despite walking on the dusty driveway.

"My friend and I are from Australia. We were hoping to get some work here."

"Australia? We have had good workers from there. Which is your friend?"

Julia pointed to Raz, who was oblivious to the exchange. "She is a very hard worker. So am I."

The man's eyes swept over her body. "Non,

non. Not you."

Julia's shoulders slumped. "I hoped there would be some light work."

"The infant, when is it due?"

"A few weeks yet."

"And the father?"

"Um...he's not..." She faltered.

"Hmm. I see." He nodded and looked at the line of workers moving slowly. "I may have something at the Chateau. I will check with my wife."

Julia looked up at the man and beamed. "Really? Oh, I'd be so grateful."

"There is a telephone in the barn. Excusez-moi."

The man disappeared into the cool-looking interior of the outbuilding. After a few minutes, he re-emerged, blinking. He walked up to the foreman and spoke in his ear, pointing to Raz. The other man nodded.

"I may have good news for you. I am Pierre, and you are...?"

"Julia."

"Enchanté." He shook her hand gently. "My wife would like to meet you. Tell your friend to come to the Chateau when she's finished the paperwork."

Julia heaved herself to a standing position and walked over to Raz.

"Hey, I might have a job at the chateau. I think you're okay for a job here, too."

"What?"

"I'll explain later. I'm going over to meet this guy's wife. He said to tell you to come over when you've done the paperwork."

"Wow. Good one! Well done!"

Pierre took Julia past the barn and onto a path

that led to the rear of the big house. There was a woman standing at the door, twisting what looked like a handkerchief between her fingers.

"Camille, this young lady is Julia."

"Enchanté."

"Hello, Camille. You have a lovely house."

"Oui. Merci. Please come in."

The three of them walked through to a small sitting room. Pierre waved his arms. "This is where we come to be informal. Someone will bring us refreshments soon."

"Oh good." Julia was fanning herself. "I'd love some water."

"Oui, of course."

Camille leaned forward. "So tell me, what has led you to us in your condition."

Julia looked at the kind and concerned faces of this husband and wife. They made her feel safe, and she didn't feel any of the paralysing shame that would normally overcome her.

"Gosh, I don't know where to start. I got pregnant in Australia."

"Didn't want your parents to know?"

"No. So my friend and I came over here."

"And what are your plans when the baby is born?" Camille looked at Pierre, who came and stood beside her.

"We thought we could leave it at a convent or something."

Camille nodded slowly and looked up at Pierre. He cleared his throat. "I think we can find you some light duties here, perhaps help with the tastings, or the tours."

"I'm afraid my French isn't very good."

"The greater percentage of the tourists speak

English, or have at least a good knowledge of it."

"Great. Raz planned to sleep in the workers quarters..."

"I think we can find you a bedroom here in the chateau. You need special consideration."

The door opened, and a trolley was wheeled in. Julia could see expensive bottles of mineral water, coated with condensation. She almost fainted at the sight.

Camille rose and poured her a glass, adding a slice of lemon. She passed it to the girl while also holding out a cloth napkin.

"Thank you. Merci."

Camille sat down again. "Tell me about the baby's father."

The door opened again and Raz was ushered in by a servant. Julia introduced her to the husband and wife. Raz nodded and smiled. Julia noticed her friend examining Pierre and Camille carefully, before looking around the room, as though searching for something.

Julia smiled at Raz. "Camille was just asking me about the father of the baby."

Raz looked at Camille. "No children of your own? I can't see any photographs."

Pierre took Camille's hand and turned to Raz. "No, we haven't been blessed."

"That's a shame. I think you'd make wonderful parents."

Julia looked at the three of them in puzzlement. It was another of those situations that she felt out of her depth in.

Raz put a hand on her friend's shoulder and squeezed it. "The father tricked Julia rather badly. He was married. We know that he was a chartered accountant with some standing in the mining industry."

"Does he know about the child?" Pierre looked like he was holding his breath for the answer.

"No. Julia didn't want him involved."

"So you are helping out your friend. That is very kind of you." Raz simply nodded.

Pierre took a baguette topped with salmon from the trolley. He offered the plate around and the two girls accepted gratefully. He wiped his mouth. "I will arrange for a twin room where the two of you can sleep. Rachel, you can help with the harvest while Julia works here in the chateau. You can both dine with us in the evenings.

Raz smiled. "And we will all get to know each other well."

"Oui. We will."

"Look at this place," said Raz in a low voice. Her eyes were round with wonder. "It looks like something out of a movie."

They were ascending the stairs slowly, looking around with awe. There was a tapestry featuring a unicorn that Julia pointed to silently. Raz nodded. Ancient-looking paintings in ornate frames hung in alcoves. The house was dark and cool.

"And they're being awfully nice to us!" Julia said. She spoke quietly, not wanting the servant who was leading the way to their room, to hear.

"Don't tell me you haven't caught on."

"To what?"

"Think about it. You've got an unwanted baby. They can't have children."

"Oh! Oh! Now I get it. So that's why you said John was a chartered accountant."

"Yeah, well, a panel-beater may not have made the grade."

"Why don't they just tell us what they want?"

"They're French. They don't do that."

"Heavens, Raz. I can't work out how you always know these things."

The door to their room was flung wide open by the servant, and she waited patiently as the girls finished mounting the stairs. Julia looked inside and clapped. "Oh, it's just lovely."

The room was lushly furnished and decorated in a style that suited the rest of the chateau. The beds looked plump and inviting, far better than the girls had experienced since leaving home months before.

Another servant brought a trolley with more food and water. He questioned them about their luggage and said that it would be collected from their accommodation and brought to them. He bowed and left.

Julia walked over to the window and stared across the vines. "I guess it would be a great place for my baby to grow up." Her voice sounded high and thin.

Raz walked over put an arm around her friend's waist. "A great place. Far better than an orphanage."

"Do you think it will be okay—my baby? Without me?"

Raz pulled Julia's hair back into a ponytail. "You hold all the cards here, you know. You can insist on things."

"How do you mean? Like what?"

"Rules. You might want updates every year. Or contact."

"Oh no. They'd have to send the updates to home—"

"But you see what I mean."

"Yeah. I get it. I don't just have to hand the baby over. I can make conditions."

"You can still decide to keep it."

"No. I won't change my mind about that." The thought of having a constant reminder of John, and what happened in the van, made her feel ill. No, she didn't want this baby.

Raz walked into the bathroom. "Wow—it's all marble. The bath is huge!"

"Are there bathrobes?"

"Yeah, and slippers. Want a bath?"

"Sure."

Julia heard the taps being turned and the water tumbling into the tub. She looked back over the vines and into the beautiful countryside. A child would be lucky to be raised there.

Julia's duties at the chateau were light. She hosted two tours per day, explaining to the round-eyed visitors, not only stories of the chateau, which featured prominently in the history of the Hundred Year War, but also what made the wines produced there unique.

When she finished each tour, she would drink a large glass of cool water from the kitchen, before moving through to the informal sitting room to read. Sometimes she wrote in her journal—reflecting on the child she was about to bear and then lose.

Sometimes Camille joined her for morning and afternoon teas, chatting away in excellent English. Julia discovered some surprising facts about Camille's past, including her degree in law and the work she had done to help vulnerable women.

Julia would watch the older woman as she talked about her work, and realise how attractive Camille's face became at these times. Helping these women was her passion and her life's work. Julia also recognised that Camille would be helping her at a vulnerable time as well, although it would be to their mutual benefit.

One day, while Julia and Camille sipped afternoon tea, Camille told the younger woman about her theory concerning friendships between women. "It has always been necessary for women to create strong friendships between themselves. Stronger than those between men. You see, from the beginning of human history, women have been vulnerable." She placed her cup on the trolley and began pacing around the room. "We're physically disadvantaged and often economically as well. These strong relationships between women provide a network of safety and support for when things go wrong. Look at you and Raz for example."

"Yes, I don't know what I'd do without her right now."

"And there will possibly be times when she'll need you. We need to be there for each other. Sadly these special friendships sometimes fracture. Women can be hurtful to each other."

Camille practised an economy of movement that fascinated Julia. Each task was undertaken thoughtfully and with a precision that harked back to another time and place. Camille was not beautiful by any means—some would call her plain—but her grace and intelligence made her an attractive woman.

In the late afternoon, Julia would walk up the stairs to her bedroom, taking each step slowly. She would undress and lower herself into the bath, where the water would rise up to her chin. Sometimes she would be so contented in this cocoon of warmth that she would have a light nap.

Raz would re-appear around that time and enter

the bedroom noisily. She would perch on the closed toilet seat, regaling her friend with stories from the day. When Julia finished in the bath, Raz would help her climb out, before undressing quickly and plunging into the same bathwater.

As the church bells pealed six times, a servant would appear wheeling a trolley. Raz would shift her weight from foot to foot until the door closed behind the departing servant and she could fall onto the food, stuffing her mouth with breads and pastries. The two girls hadn't fully understood how late the French ate their dinner until they moved into the chateau, and Raz had to endure the terrible wait until dinner was announced at precisely a quarter to ten. Julia's pregnancy was at the point where hunger wasn't too much of a problem, but for Raz it was different. She was working hard in the fields and had an appetite to match.

Dinner was the time when delicate topics were raised, but not until the food had been served and the servants dismissed. Pierre would introduce a new item for discussion and the four would each give their opinion. These topics were always about the upcoming adoption.

There was never any disagreement. No voices were ever raised even though the topics were invariably emotional ones. Julia had been well-raised and understood the system of manners that were being employed. Sometimes she would feel Raz's body tense when Pierre mentioned something that was of concern, but Julia would simply place her hand on Raz's arm. The dance of manners would continue undisturbed.

Later, when the girls had retired to their bedroom, they would discuss various aspects of the agreement that was being forged. They would decide what was needed, make notes and then Julia would calmly present her wishes during dinner the next night. By the end of the seventh dinner, full agreement had been reached.

A notary appeared the next day in time for morning tea. He was a jolly person who slurped his coffee noisily. Notes were taken, points requiring clarity raised. When he rose, he shook hands with, and congratulated, each person on their intelligent handling of the delicate matter. A contract would be drawn up for approval and signature.

And so it came to be that, one day, just as the harvest was coming to an end, and a week before her daughter was born, Julia was presented with the contract and a fountain pen. As the notary, Pierre, and Camille watched, Julia uncapped the pen and placed the nib on the dotted line. At this moment the baby kicked Julia's cervix and the discomfort caused Julia to release a slight groan. Her eyes watered. Camille rushed to her side and put a supportive arm around the Julia's shoulders. Julia became aware that Pierre was watching her with a look of alarm.

Julia took a deep breath and signed the contract, thus ensuring her child would be raised in a beautiful home by wealthy and cultured parents.

CHAPTER TWELVE

The marketplace was dusty and crowded. Raz walked swiftly, cutting a path for Julia, who was running after her. "C'mon," Raz called over her shoulder. "We don't want to miss the bus." They were forced to dodge livestock and over-zealous vendors in their determination to reach the bus station in time.

They broke into a more open area where people queued at ticket windows. Raz frowned. "Damn. This'll take a while."

Julia was breathing heavily. "I don't care if we miss it. I don't need to see any more of Turkey. We should move straight on to Greece."

"There are just a couple of places I want to see first. Okay?"

"Oh, all right."

Raz found the right queue and hopped from foot to foot while travellers ahead of her were served. Each transaction seemed to involve much talking and gesticulation. Finally, as the bus pulled into the square,

Raz was issued the tickets. The girls tumbled on board.

Julia pushed the hair back from her face. "I don't think anyone in Turkey has ever heard of air conditioning."

Raz turned and smiled. "It'll be better when the bus gets moving."

"So, what is this place all about—this one we're going to?"

"Konya? It's one of the oldest cities in the world. Great architecture. Whirling Dervishes."

"What?"

"Those guys that spin."

"Why do they do that?"

"It's a religious thing. Apparently it's amazing to see."

"Oh, okay."

The bus began moving, and the girls settled down for a long trip. Julia began reading a new novel, while Raz placed a tape in her portable cassette player and untangled her headphones. The bus bumped and swayed its way out of the town.

Raz became aware of two men who kept turning to look at them. She turned away, fighting the impulse to pull a face. One turned to the other and said something that made the second man leer.

Raz couldn't relax after that. They were young women in a country where men dominated. She looked at Julia's clothing and then her own. In the rush to pack and catch the bus, they'd dressed in clothing that would be cool and comfortable for the journey. Legs and shoulders were bare. There were only two other women on the bus and both were almost fully covered. Only their faces showed.

Raz rummaged in her backpack for a large scarf she kept there. She covered her shoulders and nudged

Julia to do the same. Her friend looked as though she was going to protest, but looked around her and then reached for her shawl. Once she was covered, Julia closed her eyes and leaned against the window.

The men were still turning to look at them and Raz was becoming increasingly disturbed. She could sense the excitement in their movements. On impulse, she drew the backpack onto her knees and rummaged inside for the pocket knife she always carried. She slipped it into the pocket of her shorts. Only then could she relax enough to close her eyes and doze.

Although it was long and tedious, the rest of the bus ride passed without incident. The countryside was interesting to Raz, who stirred from light sleep from time to time to look around. They passed through many villages where domestic animals appeared to out-number humans.

The rooms at the hostel in Konya were a disappointment. They were dirty, and there was only one bathroom to ten rooms. Raz decided that they could suffer the place for the two nights they were there.

"We'll see the Whirling Dervishes tonight and visit the museums tomorrow, okay?"

Julia shrugged. "Sure. Whatever."

Raz had been worried about her friend since they left France. It seemed that she'd left some of her enthusiasm for life back at the chateau. Maybe it was post-natal hormones. Was it a type of depression? Or was it because she'd just given away her daughter? Raz was at a loss to know how to help her.

That night they walked to the building where the Sema ceremony was to be performed. Raz read the poems of Rumi out loud as they strode down ancient streets.

There were souvenirs on sale before the performance, but the girls walked straight past those. They took their seats and waited with expectation.

The performance began with the sound of a man singing while the black-robed dancers wearing tall brown hats looked on. Gentle music from flute-like instruments played while the performers bowed to a man sitting on a rug, after which they moved on to the dance floor. Drums and other instruments joined in the music.

The dancers removed their black robes, revealing white costumes. Slowly they walked around the edge of the floor and began spinning, one at a time.

Raz was captivated. There was a feeling of intense spirituality in the atmosphere. She looked at Julia, expecting to see her absorbed in the ceremony, but just saw a look of boredom.

The spinning became faster and faster in time to the music. The dancers kept spinning and spinning until Raz expected them to start falling like bowling pins. The music reached a climax, and the dancing stopped. Raz was breathless.

"Can we go now?" whispered Julia.

Raz shook her head. There was still more to come. There was a man's voice again, more bowing. Eventually the dancers exited to the sound of celebratory music. Raz sighed.

The girls stood and filed out of the building. Raz began talking excitedly about the spectacle, but Julia just strode ahead. "It was boring. I couldn't wait to get out of there. Hey look. Everything is shut. Where will we eat?"

"I dunno. We'll walk until we find somewhere."

"We might get lost."

"Perhaps we can do without eating tonight. We've got snacks in the room."

They walked until they came to the area where their hostel was. The alley was poorly lit, and Raz was trying to find the right place.

She became aware of footsteps behind them. She didn't want to turn and look, but the furtive nature of the foot-falls compelled her to do so.

Raz turned in time to see one of the men from the bus lunging for her. She ducked and felt in her pocket, cursing because she'd changed clothes and the pocket knife was back in the room. "Run, Julia!" she screamed.

Julia, who had been oblivious to the attack to that point, turned and looked at the men. A fierce look came over her face. "What do you want?"

One of the men grinned. "Orospu." He thrust his pelvis at her.

"They don't speak English, Julia. Just run, for Christ sakes. I'll hold them off until you get away."

"No way. I'm not leaving you to fight them!"

The girls were next to each other, moving around and glaring at the men who were circling them. There was not another person in the street. "Help! Help!" cried Raz, but her voice echoed in the alleyway. She heard a window close above her and realised that nobody was going to save them.

One of the men grabbed Julia and dragged her, kicking and screaming, into an alcove. The second man made an attempt to grab Raz, but she ducked quickly and kicked him in the groin. She ran towards Julia and jumped on her attacker, holding him around the neck and poking him in the eyes. Julia stamped on his foot and then kicked him in the groin, hard. The attacker grunted loudly and doubled over. Julia brought her knee up to the man's nose and at the same time, pushed his head down. The girls heard a bone snap.

The other man got a fist-full of Raz's hair and pulled the girl to the ground. He punched her across the head, and she grunted in pain. The metallic taste of blood filled her mouth. She saw Julia come up behind the man, holding something large. It smashed against his head, and Raz had to slide across the paving stones to avoid him falling on top of her.

Julia walked across the alley and picked up another of the objects. It was a clay pot which held plants. She took it over to the alcove where her attacker lay groaning and dropped it on his head. He fell still. She began kicking him and screaming. Raz ran over and grabbed her. "Shh. Shh. We don't want trouble."

Julia shrugged Raz off and ran to the other man. She began kicking him in the head. "Stop, Julia. Now!"

"They must know where we're staying."

"So?"

"They'll come after us again."

"Okay, we'll grab our stuff and move out."

Julia moved back to the first man and stamped on his throat. "I hate these bastards." She dropped to her knees and began feeling his pockets. She produced a wad of liras and a knife. Walking over to the other man, she found the same—money and knife. "At least they can pay for a decent room." She shoved the money in a pocket and handed one knife to Raz. The other knife was clutched in her hand as she began walking away. One of the men groaned, which made her stop. It was Raz's attacker. Julia returned and kicked him once more in the groin, and twice in the head. She wiped her hands on her jeans. "They should feel lucky I didn't castrate them. Let's go."

Julia and Raz packed within minutes and ran out the back door of the hostel. Their backpacks were heavy, but when they hoisted them properly onto their shoulders, they could run fairly fast. They reached a major road and followed it until they came to a decent-looking hotel.

Raz had been looking behind them every few minutes, but could see they hadn't been followed. She and Julia stopped outside the entrance to the hotel to catch their breaths. Julia began giggling.

"What on earth are you laughing at?"

Julia was doubled over. "Those men."

"It wasn't funny!"

"It was. It's the most fun I've had in ages."

"What? You're mad. We could have been raped and had our throats slit!"

"But we didn't. It felt good to fight them."

"I must say, you were pretty cool back there. Calmly lifting pots and whacking the guys over the head. Then you picked their pockets. I think you must have had some repressed anger. I guess it's just as well—probably saved us." She began laughing too.

"Yes, I must have. All that with the baby, I think. Got rid of some negative emotions."

"So you feel better now?"

"Yes, but I hate Turkey."

"I know. We'll leave tomorrow. Greece next hey?"

"Yay! At last!"

CHAPTER THIRTEEN

Their boss at the café back in Brisbane had encouraged the two girls to visit his homeland. He, like so many, had left Greece at a young age to seek his fortune in an energetic young country.

He had suggested an itinerary which took in one of the islands and then his village on the mainland, which was situated on the Peloponnese Peninsula. "I will write my mother. You will stay with her. One week or two is okay."

The offer of free board and lodging was too good to refuse, so the girls agreed with enthusiasm, even though it meant carrying items from their boss that were presents for his parents.

Oia, on Santorini, was their first destination. The stunning village, perched on the side of a mountain with the caldera spread before it, was a delight to the girls. They rode donkeys up a steep path to their accommodation, squealing in terror. They came to know all the tiny laneways and sighed in appreciation of the incredible sunsets. They marveled at the immaculate whitewashed houses and the blue domes of the many churches.

Julia noticed a group of British people their own age in a taverna and befriended them. For a week they all socialised together. Raz was attracted to one of the young men, Ben, and spent several nights with him. Julia was left alone at these times, uncomfortable in her solitude. She had been able to swap some of her books, ones that she'd read, with the others in the group, thus ensuring a supply for some time. Raz had found a small shop that sold cassettes of American music. As their ferry left Santorini bound for Athens, both girls sighed. It had been fun but it was time to move on.

The long boat ride was an opportunity for letter writing, reading, and dozing. They composed a postcard to Amanda, who was beginning her career as a nurse and jealous of Julia and Raz's freedom. After this, the girls got bored and found the duration of the ride interminable. Even their books and music weren't enough of a distraction. They were glad to see Athens approaching and jostled to be first off the ferry.

They were met by a man of around sixty or seventy who wore a battered hat and was holding a sign saying "Julia and Rachel" in shaky capital letters. As they approached him, he beamed and gave the girls a kiss on both cheeks. He didn't speak English, so the drive to his village, two hours south of Athens, was mostly silent. This was fortunate given the state of the truck he was driving, its various noises making conversation mostly impossible.

It was nearly dark by the time they reached the farmhouse. A woman's silhouette was framed in the doorway, and she was clapping her hands and jiggling her ample frame. She grabbed Julia first, holding her by the shoulders and looking into her face. She kissed Julia's cheeks and then reached for Raz and the routine was repeated. She signaled for them to follow her.

A feast was laid out in the kitchen, which also served as the family dining area. There were skewered meats, salads, breads, and pastries, all laid out on a timber table that had ten chairs around it. There were also other dishes that the girls recognised as desserts. The woman showed them where to wash their hands, and then they all sat down for feasting.

There was little conversation—the language barrier making it mostly impossible—but the girls were thankful of that. They were hungry, and the food was delicious. They knew the word for 'thank you', *efharistó,* and used it liberally as they tasted every dish. Finally they pushed their chairs back from the table and clutched their stomachs.

Voices were heard approaching out of the darkness. The older woman rose with an exclamation and ran to greet the guests. This couple were bearing food and wine and were also exclaiming loudly. A tall figure trailed behind them. He was introduced to the farmer and his wife, and then pushed towards the girls.

"George!" the woman exclaimed.

Julia looked at the handsome man and stepped forward. "Julia, and Rachel."

George looked at them both with a smile. "Hi girls. I'm glad you're here." His accent was Australian. "You'll certainly make this village a lot more interesting."

As they approached the top of the peak, George

opened his arms and turned in a slow circle. "Look at this, girls. Isn't it amazing?"

The three of them had been hiking since daybreak. They had followed roads which became goat tracks until, further along, these tracks disappeared. They trod over low vegetation and loose rocks, until they finally approached the summit by mid-morning.

The clarity of the air made everything appear closer than it really was. There were other mountains and wide valleys. Olive groves and orange orchards created patterns on the land which took on the look of a crooked patchwork quilt. Straight roads ran through the valley, while spiral ones ascended mountains. Dark clouds hovered in the distance, but were not threatening to produce rain.

Julia and Raz drew alongside George, with Julia standing as close as she could to the tall man. The attraction between the two of them was so strong that it seemed like it had its own physical presence.

"Oh, it's beautiful, George," said Julia. "Thanks so much for bringing us up here!"

The air was cool. There were few sounds—they could hear the goat's bells and the far-off hum of farm machinery, but that was all. The quality of this near-silence was pleasing.

George sat and began unpacking the picnic that his mother had provided, the girls kneeling to help. They all sat eating quietly for a few minutes in appreciation of the fine food and views. George opened a bottle of wine with a bent corkscrew, cursing the clumsy piece of equipment.

"So, where about on the Gold Coast do you live, George?" Julia was almost batting her eyelids at him.

"At the top end. I have a used car yard. A car wash as well."

"Good businesses?"

"Yeah, great."

"They must be good if you can get away from them for a holiday here."

"I have managers I can trust—I hope!" He laughed.

Julia thought this big bear of a man was delightful. She felt tiny and protected by his presence.

"And you have a wife to watch the managers as well?"

"No. There hasn't been time for a wife. My mother insisted I come back here to find one." His face reddened. "Several girls have been paraded before me."

"Oh. Nice girls?"

"Awful." He smiled. "Not small and pretty like you, with your blonde hair and sparkling blue eyes."

"No?" Julia could see Raz's look of amusement.

"They're—well, they're not like you."

Julia looked pleased. She could hear Raz snickering behind her.

"Yes," said George. "I think you two will save me from death by boredom."

"So your mother wants you to marry a good Greek girl."

George sighed. "Yes. She's quite set on that. Says that only a Greek would be able to look after me like she does herself. I'm thirty-five!"

"It seems to be a common thing in your culture."

"Yeah." George didn't look happy about it.

Raz interrupted. "So can you be a tour guide for us? What's there to see?"

"Beautiful beaches. Ruins so ancient they will blow your mind. Fabulous seaside tavernas. All with wonderful Greek hospitality."

"Wow. You can show us all that?" Julia was batting her eyelids again.

"I am your humble servant, ladies." He bowed.

Julia and Raz looked at each other in delight. George was a godsend.

"Julia, Rachel. I've come to say goodbye!"

Julia sat up in bed and pulled a robe over her nightdress. She shivered in the fresh morning air. Raz turned over and pulled a blanket over her head.

"Coming!" Julia scampered out to the door in bare feet. A cat lazily wound its way around her legs and Julia appreciated the warmth it provided.

George's frame filled the doorway. "Here you are! I was afraid you wouldn't wake to come and say goodbye."

"Oh, I wouldn't miss it for anything. Rachel is still asleep though."

"That's fine. Let her stay there. It's you I wanted to see, anyway."

Julia beamed at him. "You'll call me when I get home then?"

"Of course. Try stopping me."

"I'm glad you don't live too far away."

"We'll have fun. I'll take you to some really nice places."

"I can't wait."

"You'll go home soon then? I don't want to wait too long."

"Yes. It's getting cold here. Time to go home for the spring."

"Good."

"You'll wait for me?"

George gave her a serious look. "Oh, yes." He

leaned forward and gave her a kiss on the lips—their first moment of passion. Julia found herself responding.

"You'd better go!"

"I'd like to stay!"

They looked at each other with longing. George's father sounded the horn of the old car and broke the spell. George began walking down to the gate. He turned and waved.

Raz joined Julia at the doorway. "He finally kissed you, hey?"

"At last."

"How did it feel?"

"Great. Like I've come alive again. I hadn't felt much since the baby, you know."

"I noticed. That's good news. I'm going back to bed."

Julia shivered. "Me too."

CHAPTER FOURTEEN

The afternoon sun was beating down on to the balcony of the hotel suite. The two girls were inside, lolling on the giant bed, enjoying the air-conditioned comfort. Both were lying on their stomachs, supported by their elbows, and both were clutching champagne glasses.

An ice-bucket stood within reach, a silent witness to their increasingly slurred conversation. A wedding dress, white and frothy, was hanging on the door frame. Every so often, one of the two girls would look at it, as though puzzled.

Julia rolled onto her back, sloshing some of the champagne onto the expensive bedding. She giggled. "I've only got a few hours of freedom left. I should be doing something."

Raz gave her a lazy smile. "Like what?"

"Something, um, risqué. A little dangerous."

"We could go out. A nightclub. Get into a little trouble."

A frown creased Julia's brow. "Then I'd have to

do make-up and hair and stuff. Can't be bothered. I'm not sure I could stand up properly anyway."

"Yeah. Me neither. Hey, how about that gorgeous porter? We could ask him to come up here for some fun when he knocks off. He could bring a friend."

"Yeah, we could all get into that giant spa," Julia waved her hand toward the bathroom, "and play around a bit."

"I can line it up, if you want."

Julia giggled. "That's the sign of a top-notch bridesmaid—ready to get the bride into trouble if she wants to."

"Yeah, could be fun."

"But I don't want to do that either." She reached for the bottle and divided the remainder between them. "Better order another bottle."

"And some food."

"Food? Oh, I suppose so. Hey, give me a kiss."

"What?"

"On the lips. I've never been kissed by a woman. That could be my risqué act."

"I dunno—"

"C'mon. Just a little one."

Raz moved commando-style across the bed, using her elbows and legs to propel herself. When she reached Julia, she brushed some hair from her face, leaned over, and kissed Julia's plump lips. Julia turned her head. "There. I've done my naughty thing. Now I can get married."

Raz moved away. "So, what did George say when you told him?"

Julia didn't reply.

"You did tell him, right? You said you would."

"Well, I tried. The words just wouldn't come."

"Jeez, Jules. I reckon it's important."

"But, he has this idea of me..."

"The innocent little bride."

"Well, yes. If I told him I'd had a baby, then I'd have to tell him about the man." Just thinking about this made the heat of shame flare in her face.

"It's better that he finds out now. What's the worst that could happen?"

"He could fall out of love with me. Call the wedding off." Tears welled in Julia's eyes.

"But don't you think that's better than him finding out after you've gotten married and had kids?"

Julia took another noisy gulp of champagne. She rolled to the edge of the bed and pulled the telephone towards her by the cord. She peered at the instructions for dialing room service. "Send more champagne, would you? Food as well. Um, don't know. Send a few dishes—finger food. Thanks." She pushed the telephone away from her until it crashed to the floor. "Anyway, it's too late now."

"You could see him tonight."

"No. We said we wouldn't see each other until tomorrow."

"That doesn't mean you couldn't—in an emergency."

"This isn't an emergency, silly."

"I think it is. Don't you see? You're going to keep this big secret from him. It'll be sort of locked up inside you. There will be this part of you he can't reach. Not good."

"Wow. I didn't think you thought about things like that. I'm impressed."

"He's such an open guy. What you see is what you get."

"Yes, that's what I like about him."

"But you—you're going to be the opposite. You're going to be all closed up." Raz held out her hand, palm upwards and then made a fist. "Like this. And that place inside you will get harder and harder to penetrate. It will end up small and impenetrable. Not good. You two have screwed, right?"

"No, I told him we had to wait until after the wedding."

"Gawd. No wonder he wanted to marry you quickly. You didn't want to…"

"No."

"So your only experience has been with John?"

Julia nodded silently.

"And I don't think you enjoyed that very much."

"No."

"I keep thinking about that morning. In the panel vans. I reckon he forced you."

Julia bit her lip. "Sort of."

"So, all I had to do was get you drunk on champagne before you'd tell me. That's tough—getting pregnant and all. Why didn't you scream or something? I would've got him off you."

Julia's mind flashed back to those few life-changing minutes; the hand over her mouth, John tearing flesh as he entered her, the feeling of powerlessness. She swallowed hard. "Couldn't. Anyway, it's history now."

"And now you have a man who will love you properly. It won't be like that, I know his type. He'll be slow and gentle."

Julia wiped each eye with the fleshy part at the base of her thumb. "I hope you're right. Hey, is the do not disturb sign still on the door?"

"Yeah, I reckon it is. I'll fix it."

Raz groaned as she lifted herself from the bed.

She picked the telephone up from the floor and put it back on the table. She opened the door and retrieved the do not disturb sign. Stretching, she rotated her hips as though she was using an invisible hula hoop. "I need to pee." She went into the bathroom and closed the door.

Julia heard the doorbell ring. She shouted, "Come in!" As she rolled over, she saw the good-looking porter wheeling in a table covered with white linen. There were delicate sandwiches, cakes, and a fruit platter. A fresh bottle of French champagne was cooling in an ice bucket.

The porter held out the leather folder containing the docket. "Will there be anything else, miss?"

Julia looked at the bill and added a large tip. She signed it messily and smiled at him. "Kiss me, will you?"

"Miss?"

"I'm getting married tomorrow." She waved toward the door frame where the frothy creation was hanging. "That's my dress. I need you to kiss me."

The porter smiled and sat on the bed next to her. He leaned over and kissed her, then began sliding his hand into her robe. Julia moved until she was just out of reach. The porter followed her. "Wouldn't you like me to...?"

The bathroom door opened and Raz stood, surveying the scene. Julia giggled. "I was just getting another last kiss. Isn't he lovely?" The porter flushed. He stood and began backing out of the room. "Thank you!" said Julia as the door closed behind him. "I'm starving all of a sudden. Let's eat!"

CHAPTER FIFTEEN

The glass doors slid apart quietly as Julia and George entered the clinic. There were three women behind a tall white desk, all young and attractive. One girl checked their details and gave them forms to be completed. Julia and George took a seat and began the task of answering questions with blue ballpoint pens that bore the name of a drug company.

Julia felt that the Gods were laughing at her. First they gave her an unplanned pregnancy after just one forced sexual encounter, and now she couldn't get pregnant after countless attempts. It had been a heartbreaking time for George and her, so they had decided to visit a fertility clinic. This was the biggest and best.

Julia had made two appointments, one for her and one for George. She wanted to talk to the specialist alone, tell him about her previous pregnancy and how it had to be kept from George. At the last minute, however, George had insisted on joining her. As she looked at the form, her heart sank. Question two: Have you ever had a pregnancy that went full-term? She ticked no. Her stomach clenched. Surely the specialist would be able to tell?

They handed the forms back and waited. Julia kept crossing and uncrossing her legs. George frowned at her, so she reached into her handbag for a book. Their names were called, and soon they were facing the doctor, who was friendly and professional.

"So I see that neither of you have had children in the past." He looked over his glasses at Julia and George. They both shook their heads solemnly. "All right. So what we begin to do now is investigate the cause of infertility. We normally start with the woman. I do a quick examination here. If I find there is nothing evident, then we usually do an internal examination under general anaesthetic. We make a small incision and pop a camera through and have a look around."

"Really?" Julia could feel she had gone pale. "What is the test for the man?"

"Oh, we just check the sperm for volume and mobility."

"So why don't you do that first?"

"Well, we'd normally at least do the first examination on the woman—the one I do here. If you pop behind that curtain there and—"

"Sorry, but I don't want to do that today." Julia could see George frowning at her. He'd be embarrassed that she was questioning a professional man of such high standing. It wasn't normal behaviour for her. "Can't you test George first?"

The specialist's brows had flown into his hairline. "Well, if you feel that strongly about it, certainly." He opened his drawer and took out a specimen bottle. "Do you want to go and do this now,

George? Or would you prefer to take it home and drop the sample back? It will be more time effective if you could do it now. I could check it while you're here and tell you the result. The receptionist will tell you what room to go to."

George had lapsed into speechlessness. He stood and took the bottle from the doctor and frowned at Julia as he left the room. Julia knew this could be a good opportunity to explain to the doctor about her previous pregnancy, but found she couldn't. The shame thing again. There was also the possibility they'd be overheard. Perhaps whatever room George had gone to shared a common wall with the doctor's room. Besides, she knew she was fertile and was banking on the fault being with George.

The specialist excused himself and left the room. Time went by. Finally, George returned. He wouldn't look at Julia, nor talk to her. After another fifteen minutes the specialist came back.

"Okay. It appears there is a problem with your sperm, George." The specialist gave Julia's husband a friendly smile. "There are two ways of treating this. We'll try the easy one first." He reached into the drawer of a filing cabinet and extracted a sheet of information. "Try this vinegar douche before intercourse. If it doesn't work, we can try in-vitro fertilisation. It's just new, but we're achieving good results."

As they walked out of the building, Julia tucked her hand in to George's big one. He didn't resist. "Thanks for that," she said. "I didn't want him touching me down there. I'd be embarrassed. Especially with you just behind the curtain. I don't like anybody touching me there other than my big, hairy man." Julia was relieved to see a smile tugging at the corners of George's mouth.

Julia had just dodged a big bullet. She'd been very lucky.

CHAPTER SIXTEEN

"Wow!" said Raz. "You didn't tell me it was this nice."
She walked through to the back of the house where
steps led down to a pontoon which floated on the canal.
There was a decent-sized leisure cruiser tied up there.
"That is yours too, I suppose."

Julia shrugged. "George's. Not mine. It's his
baby."

"Don't like boating, then?"

"No, it's boring. All the boating crowd here are
awful. I hate it."

"And the boys. Do they like going cruising with
their Dad?"

"Of course. George is great with them. Has
taught them to fish. They get so excited."

Julia showed Raz the rest of the house. "Plenty
of bedrooms now. You can come and stay whenever
you want."

"Nah. It's not a long drive from Brisbane.
Besides, I don't think George would want me here

much."

"I don't care. You're my friend and you're always welcome."

The two women smiled at each other. They moved into the kitchen, where Julia selected a bottle of bubbling wine from the refrigerator and two glasses from a cabinet. She handed a platter of food to Raz, and they moved out to the deck.

"So what's so awful about the boating crowd?"

"They're such snobs. One of the nicer neighbours asked me to her place for morning tea, not long after we moved in. She also invited another six neighbours—all boaties. I'll never forget it, those cows."

"Cows?"

"The women. Anne, who invited me, was okay, but the others were such snobs. Fortunately, I'd been to the right schools and had a good background. One said, "You're husband—he's a *used car salesman* isn't he?" I said, "He did have a used car business at one stage. Now he's a motor dealer with three luxury brands. He employs two hundred people." That put her back in her place."

Raz laughed. "Now I know why you call them cows."

"Then there was another time we went for lunch—eight of us, all women. A minor celebrity in the US had just released the information that thirty or so years ago she'd given up an illegitimate baby for adoption. These women were scathing of her—calling her a heartless bitch."

"That must've hurt."

Julia remembered the feeling this had caused in her—the shame which engulfed her all over again. "Yes. The problem is that George wants me to be tight with this group—says it will help the business. I can't stand them."

"So, other than Anne, there's no one nice around here?"

"There's a guy. Lives three doors down. His wife left him six months ago and took the kids. He seems nice enough. The women are always talking about him, always making up excuses to drop in and visit. I think they all fancy him."

"So they're bitches who are also desperate. Bad combination."

Julia laughed. Raz always made her feel so good about herself. "But I'm getting good at pretending to like them. All those air kisses and falseness. I can do that."

"I guess it's a small price to pay for this lifestyle."

"True, but I never asked for all of this." Julia waved her arm around, taking in the house, the boat and the expensive suburb. "Sometimes I just wish for a simpler life."

George finished the last mouthful of dessert and pushed his chair back from the table. "Good news. We won that dealer of the year award I was telling you about. Means a lot."

Julia viewed his swelling abdomen with distaste. "That's great. Congratulations."

"Hey, you need congratulating too. I know you do good work behind the scenes. That charity thing you organised was damned good. It gave us a lot of positive publicity."

Julia's own body was toned and taut, thanks to daily gym workouts. When she'd tried to get George interested in doing some exercise, he'd shown a total lack of interest. "Time is money. I don't have time for that," he'd said. Now he was becoming obese. It was affecting how Julia felt about him physically. There was only a certain amount of pretending a person could do in their daily life, and Julia had reached her limit.

"So, what do you get for this prize?"

"Lots of publicity from the manufacturer, a fat bonus cheque, and a trip to Europe. You'll like this one."

"Oh?" Julia's heart began sinking.

"Yeah. It's for a month. Orient Express, Mediterranean cruise, tour of Paris. Wait 'til you see the details."

"Tell me there aren't a lot of formal dinners."

George frowned. "Um...yes. I'll need my tux." He patted his belly. "We might have to get it altered. You'll need some gowns."

The last dealer trip had been a nightmare for Julia. She remembered thinking about how much happier she'd been travelling with Raz on limited money. She wished she could just say no, she wasn't going. A thought occurred to her. "What about the boys? A whole month without us?"

"Already sorted. Mum and Dad will take them." George had brought his parents to Australia and set them up in a home not far from where he and Julia were living.

"But their school events and things. Will your parents be able to cope?"

"Maybe one of your friends who has kids at their school will be able to help with the day to day stuff. Could you ask?"

"Sure."

"I really need you on this trip. You know how to schmooze the manufacturers. Nobody does it as good as you."

Julia nodded and began clearing the table with the slowness of someone in the last stages of drowning.

Julia looked at her new mobile telephone, which was sitting on the kitchen bench. When George first gave it to her, she felt touched that he'd thought to do such a thing. Now it was the enemy—it meant he could keep tabs on her.

"Mum! Mum!" The back door slammed.

"Hi Costas. Remember to close the door quietly. Where is Nicholas?"

"Aw, he walks too slowly. Wants to look at bugs and stuff."

"You must be patient with him, Costas. He's younger than you. I need you to look out for him." She gave him a hug. "You're my big boy. My little man."

Costas wiggled with delight. He loved her calling him that.

"Go and see where Nicholas is. Okay?"

Costas ran out of the house making the sound of a revving engine. Julia looked at the mobile telephone again. It rang, making her jump.

"Hello?"

"Hey, it's me. I'm ringing from a telephone box."

Julia's heart began racing. "Hello, you."

"I was just thinking of that gorgeous body of yours. I've only just made love to it, but already want you again. You're making me insatiable."

Julia groaned. He knew just the right words.

"And not only that. I think I'm falling a little in love with you."

"Don't even think it. I'm a married woman and a mother."

"I know, but I just can't help it. I dream about us being together. When can I see you next?"

The boys ran into the kitchen and began attacking the pantry for snacks. Julia moved into the living room.

"Um...maybe Friday?"

"That long, hey? Damn."

"Well, maybe Thursday, around lunchtime?"

"Can't do Thursday. Friday it is then. One o'clock?"

"Sure."

"Can't wait. I'm going to do things to you that'll make you scream."

"In a good way, I hope."

"You'd better believe it."

She terminated the call and realised there was another call coming through. George.

"Julia? Julia?"

"Hello George."

"I tried to call you earlier but the mobile was switched off."

Julia bit her lip. "It must've been while I was buying petrol."

"Oh, okay. Everything okay?"

"Great. I've got lamb for dinner."

"Can't wait. Thanks, honey. See you later."

Julia rose from the sofa and adjusted the cushions. She heard the television roar to life and frowned. "Turn it down, boys!"

She felt like some wine or a cigarette or something.

Anything.

Julia slid her plate aside and reached for Raz's

sunglasses, removing them so she could see her friend's eyes when she spoke to her.

"I've got something to tell you."

"Very dramatic indeed. This'll be good."

The restaurant was busy in a chaotic sort of way, and some diners waited a long time for service, but it was worth it for the food. It was a favourite of Julia and Raz's, being a traditional Greek taverna near Julia's house. They enjoyed sitting outside in the winter sunshine.

Julia took a sip of her wine. "I don't know where to start."

"You have a lover."

"How did you know?"

"I guessed some time ago. What's he like?"

"Gorgeous, sexy, smooth. Deep voice."

"Not big and hairy like George?"

"Quite the opposite."

"Hmm. A ladies man?"

"He says he's only seeing me."

"What does he do?"

"Investment banking."

"I see. Single?"

"Yes, his wife left last year."

"Ah, so this is the neighbour guy that has all the women lusting after him. Why did his wife leave?"

"Don't know."

Raz nodded slowly. "Serious?"

"He says he's falling in love with me."

"What about you?"

"I'm crazy about him. Can't sleep or eat. I can't even concentrate on reading a book anymore."

"Sounds like love—or infatuation."

The waitress was blonde and perky, not Greek at all. She cleared their plates away.

"There's more." Julia brushed her forehead with the back of her hand. "He's being sent to Hong Kong."

"Oh, so no more Mr. Smooth guy?"

"I'm thinking—"

"Hmm?"

"I'm thinking of going with him."

Raz raised her eyebrows. "Really?"

"Contemplating it."

"Jeez, Jules. That's a biggie."

It wasn't often that Julia saw Raz taken aback. It made tears well in her eyes. "You're the most non-judgmental person I know, other than Christopher. I hoped—"

"That I'd say it's okay to leave George? Well, yes. I know you've been unhappy for a long time. But what about the boys? Don't forget my father left my mother and me."

"Yeah, but you haven't really spoken about it. I didn't realise it meant much to you."

"Of course it did. It always does with little kids. You're their whole world."

"Damn it, Raz."

"I didn't stick to the script, did I? You wanted me to give you permission."

Tears began running down Julia's cheeks. "I hoped you'd understand."

"But you see, I understand perfectly. It's you that doesn't get it."

"How do you mean?"

"You have a man that adores you and two children who think the sun shines out of your arse. You are well-provided-for and never have to worry about how to pay bills or put food on the table." She paused for breath. "This wasn't enough for you. Boredom set in and you found a lover. That wasn't enough—"

"Hey!"

"It's all true. You're not getting enough attention from poor George who works so hard to keep his family provided for, so you want out. Your lover gives you all his attention a couple of times a week, for how long? Two or three hours?"

Julia lifted her chin. "About that."

"So he has become your hero."

"I love him."

"It sounds like you've already made up your mind."

"Maybe."

"Has he asked you?"

"What?"

"To go with him?"

"Not in so many words. But if he loves me like he says—"

"Well, here's my advice. Before you decide too much, make sure he's keen for you to go."

"I'm sure he is."

"But make sure. Then if he's keen and you're keen, then I guess there'll be no stopping you."

"You won't think too badly of me?"

"Nah. It's your life. Do what you want." Raz turned and looked out the window. Julia watched her carefully.

"What about you? How's it going with that new guy—the musician?"

"Didn't take. There's another one. He's in advertising."

"He must be keeping you up nights. You look tired." Julia examined her friend. "In fact, you look like crap."

Raz reached for her sunglasses and replaced them. "Yeah, just tired."

"Your skin is sort of yellowish. What does that mean? Liver?"

"Dunno."

"You've always drunk too much. Nothing else, is there?"

"Like what?"

"Drugs or anything."

"What makes you say that?"

"Because you're so thin, and when I took your sunglasses off before, your pupils looked weird."

"Doesn't mean anything." Raz stood. Reaching into her back pocket, she pulled out money that she threw on the table. "Gotta go."

"Keep your money. My shout."

Raz shook her head. "Let me know what you decide about Hong Kong."

"If I go, I'll miss you dreadfully."

Raz smiled at her friend, an expression that didn't portray happiness. "Me too, darling. Me too."

Time moved slowly for Julia. Philip's departure date was looming, and each time they met, he would talk about how he would miss her, and discuss ways they would stay in touch. He said he wouldn't be gone more than twelve months—he just had to set up the Hong Kong office, hire staff, and get things running smoothly. He'd be very busy.

She had waited for the smallest opening that could lead to a discussion about her accompanying him to his new posting. As each day passed, she became increasingly frustrated. If she were to go, there would be so much to do. She'd need flights. Clothes. She'd have to plan how best to escape.

One day she thought about her passport. Where was it? George took care of those sorts of documents, and she was fairly certain he'd have it locked away somewhere. She strode into the spare bedroom he called his study and began opening and closing drawers, each one more quickly than the last. After more than fifteen minutes of frustration, she gave up and returned to the dining table to sit and stare into the rose garden.

When Julia had told George she wanted a rose bed to supply fresh-cut flowers for the house, he had instructed the gardener to plant as many bushes as it would take for her to have a bountiful supply. From her seat at the table she saw the blooms dying on their branches. She just didn't care—couldn't raise enough energy to go and collect any.

The state of affairs with Philip was causing her to see negatives in all aspects of her life. Julia slammed her fist on the table-top. Nothing was going right. Tears of self-pity welled in her eyes.

She thought about the previous week. A package had arrived at the post office box, the secret one she had arranged just so Emilie's parents could send six-monthly updates on the child's progress. She had sat in her luxury car, in her exclusive canal suburb, and read the report with tears dripping onto the page. She had shoved the envelope into her handbag and driven home so that she'd be able to down a scotch while she re-read the tightly written lines with shaking hands. Emilie was turning into a young woman. Soon she would be getting her first period. Julia would miss all of this. She began sobbing.

When George arrived home that night, it was to a half-drunk and upset wife who refused tell him what was wrong. Since then, she'd often look up to find his eyes on her, his face a picture of puzzlement.

The mobile telephone chirped. It was Philip. He

wanted to see her on Friday. She looked at the message and sighed. What was to be done?

CHAPTER SEVENTEEN

The driver was looking in his rear-vision mirror from time to time, and this was disturbing Julia. She shunted over to the other side of the car and wiped her eyes.

It was done. She'd left a note for George in his study, wedged between the keys of his computer keyboard. She'd driven the boys to school, taking them to a park on the way. They'd all sat in a row on a bench, with her in the middle. She told them she had to go away for a little while.

Costas had tugged her sleeve. "Where?"

"Oh, a little way away. But it won't be for too long."

"Who will take care of us?"

"Dad will. He's good at that."

Nicholas had stared at her mutely. His bottom lip had begun to wobble. She had taken them the rest of the way to school and spoken to each of their teachers. All she'd told them was that she had to go away and that George would be making arrangements for the boys' care. Both teachers nodded and didn't comment further.

There was only one more thing to do, and she'd do it from the airport just before boarding. She'd send George a text message to tell him to collect the boys from school.

Then her duties would be fulfilled. She would be free.

She dialed Raz's number. A sleepy voice answered. "Hello?"

"Aren't you out of bed yet?"

"Jeez. What time is it, Jules?"

"Eleven. Late night?"

"Yeah. What's up?"

"I'm on my way to the airport." Julia heard a sharp intake of breath.

"So he eventually asked you?"

"No. I know why, too. He didn't think he had the right to ask. Didn't want to be the cause of a bust-up."

"But he is expecting you?"

"No. I'm going to surprise him!"

Raz groaned. "Jules, Jules."

"He'll be so happy to see me!"

"Do you know his address?"

"No, but the new office will be easy to find."

"So, you'll check into a hotel then find him. Right?"

"Um, I guess so."

"Okay. Let me know how it goes, hey?"

"Sure. How are you?"

"Fine."

"No, I mean it. How are you?"

"I'm fine!"

"If you get yourself sorted out, you could come to Hong Kong and visit."

"What do you mean by sorting myself out?"

"Don't make it hard, Raz. You know what I mean."

"The funny thing about you, Julia, and I've noticed it before, is that despite the fact you've cheated on your husband and have now left him for another man, you still come across as a total innocent. You look and sound as fucking pure as the driven snow. I just don't get it."

Julia felt anger rising. Where had that come from? How dare Raz criticize her? She decided not to react, however. She didn't want to argue with her friend.

"I'm just lucky, I guess."

"I remember when you and George began dating, back here in Australia. He treated you like a virginal princess."

"Yes, I remember."

"I think he still believes that of you. This will hit him hard, you know."

Julia began sniffing again. "I know."

"How did the boys take it?"

"Oh, okay. I told them I wouldn't be gone long."

"Hmm. Maybe you won't either. Give me a call after you find your man, hey?"

"Sure."

Julia craned her neck to look up the ultra-modern building that housed Philip's new Hong Kong office. It was located in the Central district on Hong Kong Island, and Julia had arranged a car and driver to take her there. She didn't want to walk from the hotel in the heat and humidity.

She knew she should move into the building

quickly before the atmosphere began taking its toll on her hair and makeup, but hesitated. Should she have let him know? Was surprising him such a good idea after all?

She heard the car pulling away from the kerb behind her, and that made her decide to move forward. She entered the building, shivering as the refrigerated air made contact with her moist skin.

The elevators were confusing, and it took several minutes to locate the right one. She gasped as the floors shot past and the walls became glass, and she was treated to a panoramic view across Hong Kong.

As the elevator doors opened, she stepped out and bit her lip. She consulted the note in her hand, realising she had been clutching it so hard that it was now crumpled and damp. Turning left, she followed the corridor around until she came to the correct office.

The receptionist was a doll-like Chinese girl who spoke impeccable English. Yes, she was in the right place but Mr. Anderson wasn't there. He had called in saying he was taking the afternoon to attend to personal business. No, she could not give Julia his home address or telephone number. Was Mr. Anderson expecting her? No? Would Julia like her to contact him? No?

Julia could sense an attitude in the girl, as though Philip needed protection from people like herself. It made her angry and she could sense humiliation rising. A blush was creeping up to her face.

"Look. This isn't a big deal, okay? I'm just a friend passing through Hong Kong. I remembered Philip saying he was setting up an office here. I'd like to surprise him, so please don't tell him I've been here."

"Of course not, Madam." Was there a note of

sarcasm in the girl's tone, or was Julia imagining it?

"I'll call back in the morning, unless Philip has another engagement?"

"I cannot guarantee he will be here, but you are more than welcome to return then."

At the base of the building, a blast of hot air felt like it was going to suffocate her. Why didn't she keep the car and driver until she was sure about Philip? She waved her arms at several taxis, but they drove straight past. Where was her hotel? The car had approached the building from the left, so she began walking in that direction.

After only a block she felt like sitting on the footpath and crying. There was a small café or restaurant across the road, so she dodged traffic until she was standing in front of it. The inside looked dirty and the booths had vinyl seats, but she needed time to calm down.

The laminated menu was standing in a metal holder. She decided on a cup of tea and ordered it from an ageing Chinese woman who walked with a bent back. A few moments later it was served to her without ceremony.

She sipped from the cup and evaluated her position. Nothing had gone to plan, but that didn't mean it wouldn't in the future. As soon as she was reunited with Philip, things would be perfect. She felt her strength returning, and, with it her customary positive attitude.

This time, as she stepped from the restaurant, there was a taxi ready to take her to the hotel. She could fill the afternoon by having some beauty treatments. She would eat dinner in the lobby restaurant and have an early night so as to look fresh for Philip the next day. Yes, that was a perfect plan.

The receptionist was talking to what looked like a co-worker as Julia approached the next morning. The second girl was Caucasian, with auburn hair and porcelain skin.

Julia fixed a smile on her face and said a bright, "Good morning."

"Good morning, Madam."

Julia waited for the receptionist to give some sign of recognition, or to tell her Philip's whereabouts, but the girl was looking at her expectantly.

"Is Philip in this morning?"

"I will check for you. Your name is?"

The fact the girl had asked her name this time probably meant he was in the office. Julia's heart began drumming a fast beat. She gave the receptionist her name, while the second girl watched Julia with curiosity. The receptionist spoke quietly for a few seconds and then pressed a button.

"If you take a seat, Mr. Anderson should be out in a moment."

Julia sat and looked around her. There were magazines on a table beside her seat, but they were all about business and finance. She sat with her hands in her lap. After a few moments she realised she was clasping and unclasping her fingers. She slid her hands under her thighs.

"Julia! Heavens! What are you doing in Hong Kong?"

Philip was standing before her with a quizzical expression on his face. Was he glad to see her? Julia couldn't judge. She looked towards the two girls behind the reception desk and saw they were watching Philip and her with expressions of interest.

"I, um...I was passing through—"

"Passing through Hong Kong? That must've been sudden!"

"Yes, well it was." She dropped her voice. "Is there somewhere...?"

Philip looked around and noticed the two employees. "Yes, of course. Come out here." She expected him to take her into an office, but instead he clutched her elbow and led her into the corridor.

As the door shut, she turned until she was squarely in front of him and could see his eyes. "I've left George. I've come to be with you."

If anything, Philip's face became devoid of expression. He breathed slowly and then looked down at his feet.

"You should have spoken to me first, Julia."

"I wanted to surprise you."

"Yes, yes. I understand, and it's a nice surprise. You've just caught me at a bad time."

"You're busy, I suppose."

"Very. Where are you staying?"

"I've checked out of the hotel. My luggage is in a car downstairs. If you give me your address and the keys, I could go to your place and wait for you."

"Hmm. Yes, but I think we can work out a better plan. Come back inside and take a seat. I just need to do a few things."

They moved back into the reception area and Philip waved Julia into the chair. He motioned to the redhead behind reception. "Bonnie, can I see you for a moment?" She followed him into the rear of the office, and after a few minutes Julia could hear raised voices. The receptionist grimaced. Bonnie came running past Julia and shot her a hostile look before leaving by the main doors.

Philip came back. "You say there's a car and driver downstairs? Excellent. Let's go for a drive."

CHAPTER EIGHTEEN

"Did you ever see the movie, *Love is a Many Splendored Thing*?" Philip's expression was calm as he looked down at the beach.

"Um, no. I don't think so."

"Great old motion picture. They shot the beach scene here, I think. This is Repulse Bay."

"Oh, I see. So where is your apartment?"

"Patience, dear Julia. We'll go there soon. Aren't you interested in seeing Hong Kong?"

"Yes, but I'm more interested in seeing you."

"Which you are. I'm right here."

"I thought you might want to make love to me. It's been weeks." Julia felt her eyes filling with tears.

"Yes, of course. How lovely of you. We'll go there soon." He leaned forward. "Stanley, please driver."

Although the views were scenic, Julia wasn't enjoying herself. "What's at Stanley?"

"Oh, it's quite lovely. Promenade, restaurants. I

want to take you to a nice restaurant for lunch before we go back to my place."

"I could make you something—"

"No food in the house. Typical bachelor pad." He laughed.

"I'll make it more of a home for you."

"Lovely, lovely."

Philip pointed out landmarks until they came to Stanley. He asked the driver to wait, telling him they might be gone for an hour or so. He led Julia to a seafood restaurant with views over the bay. They were seated quickly, and Philip ordered for both of them.

"What was wrong with that Bonnie girl?"

"Who?"

"That girl in your office. The redhead. She gave me a filthy look when she ran out."

"Um, I don't know. She's been having trouble with her boyfriend. Must be that."

Julia stabbed her fish with a fork, which made contact with the plate, causing a screeching sound. She thought it sounded like a scream.

Philip shot her a look. "Don't like the fish?"

"No, it's not that. I had a late breakfast."

"So tell me what happened when you left George."

"Not much. I just left him a note."

"I see. He must be shocked. Has he tried contacting you?"

"I don't know. He didn't know where I was staying and I've had my mobile switched off."

"Why?"

"Because of the calls I'm expecting."

"I see. What did you tell George in the note?"

"I told him about you."

"Perhaps you shouldn't have done that."

"Why not?"

"Burning bridges, that sort of thing."

Julia shrugged. "I didn't think that mattered. I was coming to be with you and I wanted to be honest about it."

Philip ate the last few mouthfuls of food. He looked at his watch. "Time to go."

The car made its way back towards the city. Eventually they pulled up at another very tall building. Philip helped Julia out of the car while the driver retrieved the luggage from the rear. Julia stood, clutching her handbag grimly. Philip put his hand on the small of her back and led her through the automatic glass doors.

"The company have rented the penthouse here for a few months until I get myself another place."

"I thought you were only staying a year."

"It may be longer now."

They stood in the lift in silence. Julia felt misery washing over her, knowing that something was broken. She frantically searched her brain for ways to fix it. Once they got into bed...

Philip opened one of the double penthouse doors almost hesitantly. He motioned to Julia to stay still while he entered alone. He returned in a minute or so with a smile. "I just had to check the cleaning lady had done her job well." He waved her in.

The view was outstanding. Julia stood against the high windows and watched the bustle of Hong Kong happening below. She heard Philip's mobile telephone ringing.

"Hello? Oh really? What, right now? No, I was busy, but if it's that important. Sure. See you soon." He looked at Julia with a crooked smile. "I'm needed urgently. Must run. See you later." He gave her a kiss on the cheek and ran out of the apartment.

Julia's pose was that of a person who'd just had cold water tipped over them. She stood like that for several minutes before straightening her shoulders and beginning the process of unpacking.

At some point, hours later, she realised she was marooned in the apartment. Philip hadn't given her keys, so she didn't dare leave. There was little food in the refrigerator and cupboards, and what was there didn't look too fresh.

She used Philip's land line to call Raz and gave her a quick report that glossed over the facts. Her friend had been right all along, but Julia didn't want to admit it. She used the excuse of the call costing Philip a great deal, then hung up quickly. She didn't even ask how her friend was.

It was dark before she heard the click of the door. She ran to greet Philip, who looked grey from tiredness. He was carrying containers of food.

"You didn't leave me a key. I couldn't do any shopping."

"No problems. I'll get another one cut."

Julia searched the kitchen for crockery and cutlery while Philip changed out of his suit. She found a bottle of white wine in the refrigerator and opened it. When he came out, he smiled. "Lovely. We'll be able to look over the lights of the city while we eat."

He told her about the events of the afternoon, which she didn't find interesting. They listened to music. Philip fell asleep on the sofa and she woke him, telling him they should move into bed.

At one stage through the night she rolled onto her stomach and thrust an arm under the pillow. Her fingers encountered something that shouldn't have been there and she pushed it out of the bed wearily before returning to sleep. It wasn't until next morning, after she'd woken to find Philip already dressed and leaving for work without breakfast, that she thought of it. She looked down the crack between the bed and the bed-head and saw something green. She reached down until her fingers touched it and then hauled it upwards. Lingerie, green and lacy, clearly left for her to find.

Philip still hadn't shown any interest in making love to her. Her stomach squeezed into a knot.

In the week that followed, Julia felt that karma was in force against her. Philip was remote. When she eventually turned on the mobile telephone, it was to messages that made her feel ill. George was in tears with Costas and Nicholas howling in the background. Her mother and father were taking turns to tell her what a selfish brat she was. Christopher, her brother, was laughing and saying that at least life wasn't boring around her. George again, asking her to please reconsider for the sake of their children.

Philip would leave each morning before she woke and return after dark. He didn't call her during the day. He'd left her a set of keys, but his apartment was some distance from shopping centres, and it was difficult to bring groceries home. She was isolated and lonely. When she suggested that Philip introduce her to his friends, he told her he hadn't made any yet, had been too busy working.

Reading had been a refuge for Julia since childhood, but even this had deserted her. She would scan the pages, turning them quickly, then realise she had no idea of what had happened in the story. She would flick back to where she had started from and repeat the process all over again. One day she threw her book into a corner, where it remained unread.

She had only given the land line number to two people, Christopher and Raz. When the telephone rang one day, it was so unexpected that it made her jump.

"Hello."

"Hey, sis. It's me."

"Hey. How are Mum and Dad now? Have they calmed down?"

"I'm not ringing about them. It's Raz."

"Huh?"

"Raz. She's in hospital—in a bad way. Apparently she gave them your details as next of kin."

"Really? What about her mother?" Julia searched her memory and couldn't remember Raz mentioning her mother for a long time.

"Don't know. Anyway, they've been trying to contact you—rang Mum. She rang me."

"I see. Has Raz been in an accident?"

"Nup. Apparently she's just really sick. Liver and other things."

"Oh, gosh."

"I don't know what you can do from there, but I had to let you know. Can you call the hospital?" He gave her the details.

"Sure. I'll call them right away."

"Everything okay there?"

"Um, yes. Fine. Are you good?"

"Yep. Call them."

"Will do."

She hung up and then called the hospital in Brisbane. It seemed to take forever to be put through to the ward sister. Julia listened to what the woman had to say and then hung up and called several airlines until she got a flight that evening. She packed quickly and went to leave the apartment. As she stood at the door, she wondered about leaving a note, but then she had another thought. She retrieved the green lacy knickers from where she'd hidden them in a drawer. She went to the dining table and arranged them dramatically over a candle-holder. She then walked out the door with her head held high.

In the years that followed, when her memory was prompted about Hong Kong, whether it was in social conversations or through the media, she wouldn't recall the sights and sounds of that city. She would just remember the horror of realising she'd made a mistake, the stress that caused physical discomfort, and the isolation of being in a foreign country without a friendly guide.

She never heard from, nor contacted Philip again.

CHAPTER NINETEEN

Julia stood in front of the sink, washing dishes in the morning sunshine. When the sun shone on one of the bubbles, making it glisten with rainbow colours, she smiled. How long had it been since she'd felt so happy? Probably not since she and Raz were travelling through Europe.

Everything made her smile these days, even performing menial tasks that she hadn't had to do in the time she was married to George. Her existence was simple now. She cooked, cleaned, shopped, washed, and cared for Raz. What's more, she did this with an open heart. Never before in her life had she acted so unselfishly, putting another person's needs before her own. Perhaps she was growing up, she mused.

Hearing a rustling of bedclothes, she pulled the rubber gloves from her hands and poured a glass of water. She took a bottle of tablets from a shelf and carried them, with the water, into the bedroom.

"Good morning!"

Raz lifted her head. "Hey."

"Do you want me to open the curtains?"

"Sure, but slowly."

"Wait until you see this day. It's glorious."

She waited until Raz covered her eyes before gently tugging at the curtains. The bedroom filled with light. She sat on the bed and put two tablets in Raz's hand.

Raz hoisted herself into a sitting position and swallowed the medication. She smiled at Julia.

"Thanks."

"You're welcome. Did you sleep well?"

"Yeah, feel heaps better."

"Great. One day soon, when you're up to it, we'll pack a picnic lunch to eat in the sunshine. Perhaps down by the river."

"Cool. I'm sure I'll be up for it soon."

"I'm sure, too. I'm amazed at how well you're recovering."

"Only because of how you're taking care of me. I don't know how I would have managed, by myself."

When Julia thought of how Raz looked when she'd first visited her in hospital, she found it hard to believe this was the same person. Back then she'd cried, taking Raz into her arms and sobbing into her hair. Her friend had consisted of just skin and bone, a condition brought on by a severe form of hepatitis as well as an addiction to prescription drugs. Julia didn't know that when she'd rung Raz from Hong Kong, her friend was already very ill and had collapsed in the street the day after.

Julia had come to Raz's apartment, thinking she could stay there until Raz was released from hospital, but what she found there turned her stomach. For a week she worked hard and transformed the apartment into something liveable. She burned the bedding and towels, and threw out the floor rugs. She scrubbed and mopped and wiped and vacuumed until surfaces shone. She emptied cupboards and began stocking them afresh.

She found unpaid bills and arranged payment, still using the credit card that George had provided. She realised that this would alert him to the fact she was back in Brisbane, but didn't have the time or energy to contact him.

When Raz was released into her care, Julia nursed her with patience and hard work. Gradually, Raz's condition improved, and they were both able to sleep for long stretches. Raz's specialist had been astounded at the rapid recovery.

Looking at her friend now, Julia was proud of what she had achieved. "Breakfast! Eggs on toast?"

"Hey, yeah. And how about blueberries and yogurt?"

"Fresh squeezed orange juice?"

"Yum. And green tea."

"In here?"

"You know what? I reckon I could make it out to the table."

"Brilliant!"

Over breakfast, Julia wanted to tell Raz about the thoughts she'd had while doing dishes—about the unselfish life and how it filled her with joy, but she couldn't. The words just wouldn't come. She smiled and kept her thoughts to herself.

Julia was at the pharmacy, getting more prescriptions filled for Raz. She was tired and rushed. So much to do.

The   pharmacist   came   from   behind   the

dispensary to ask her questions about her knowledge of the drugs being supplied and how to administer them. Julia answered the questions coherently, then sat to wait. She felt her mobile telephone vibrate in her pocket, and panicked, thinking something was wrong with Raz.

It was George's number. Julia bit her lip and considered diverting the call to voicemail. She wanted to be the one to contact George, not the other way around. On impulse she pressed the green button.

"Hi Julia. You're back."

"Hi. Yes, I am."

"I can see by the credit card statements that you're in Brisbane. Things didn't work out with your new man, then?"

Julia analysed his tone and words for traces of satisfaction or sarcasm. There weren't any. This made her want to be honest with him. "No, it wasn't going well. Then Christopher rang to say Raz was seriously ill. I came home to look after her."

"I see. So, what are your plans then—when Raz recovers? Are you coming home to the boys and me?"

"Um…no. I don't think so. I just don't think I can do that. You must have known that I wasn't happy there. I hadn't been for a long time. "

"That's the thing you see. I didn't know. Had no idea, and I guess that was part of the problem. We can fix that—can make whatever changes necessary to make you happy. I'll do anything. I can work fewer hours. I'll lose weight and get fitter. We can see counsellors—"

"I don't think…"

"Please Julia. For the boys' sakes if not for mine. Please. At least give it a go. Just try it."

Julia hated the tone in his voice, hated the fact

she'd reduced this strong and capable man to someone who had to plead with her. "No, George. I'm truly sorry, but I don't think I can do that. When Raz is better, I'll find a place of my own and then we'll talk about the boys. They'll live with me, of course. You can see then whenever you want."

Julia heard a sharp intake of breath at the other end. There was a moment of silence, then a sound as though George had slammed his fist against something, maybe a filing cabinet. "Tell me you're not serious. Tell me you don't really believe you can just take the boys from me. After all you've done, you think you can just remove them from their home and take them away? Then I suppose you'll find a new man and they'll be raised by him?"

George's voice was cracking. Julia bit her lip, realising she hadn't considered his feelings in all of this. He was talking again. "I won't allow this, Julia. Listen to me carefully. I will fight you through any means and in any court I can. Do you really think anyone would grant you custody? Really? A mother who abandons her children to go away with another man. She comes back but then doesn't make any contact with them in how long? Weeks? Do you really think they would consider you a fit and caring mother?"

"But—"

"No buts, Julia. I'm serious. You are not taking them from me."

"How would you look after them?"

"The same way I have been since you left. I'm spending less time at the dealerships. My parents fill in where needed. The boys' teachers and other parents have been helping."

"I'd need to see them."

"Of course." George's voice softened.

"Naturally you'll see them. Whenever you want. When you get your own place you can have them on weekends and school holidays."

Julia had been pacing the floor of the pharmacy while talking to George. Now her legs felt weak. She had to sit. The full understanding of her situation had just hit. She was going to be the parent without custody. The one who plays only a minor role in their children's rearing. This is what she had brought on herself by immaturity and naivety.

She became aware that George had begun talking again. "Or you could simply come home again. We would raise wonderful children, maybe have another baby, and grow old together. Wouldn't that be better?"

Julia closed her eyes and tried to imagine life back with George. Just the thought of that suffocating lifestyle made her heart beat faster. Her breathing became shallow and rapid. Walls seemed to be closing in. She felt faint and sick. She wondered if she were having a panic attack.

"Well?"

Julia found her voice again. "I'm so sorry, George. I just can't do that. I appreciate the fact you have even offered to take me back after what I did. Most men would tell me to go to hell. You're an amazing man and have been a brilliant husband. Whoever ends up with you will be a lucky lady."

"I see."

"I'll keep in touch. The boys—I'll see them next week. I know you'll be more than fair with me. Thank you…"

Julia's voice trailed off and she terminated the call before George could say anything else. She wiped her eyes and sat, staring at the floor. Eventually her name was called. She stood automatically and approached the counter. Raz would be waiting. Life would go on. That's just the way it was.

Raz came through the door breathlessly. "Hey, I think I've found it!"

"What?"

"The café."

Julia looked up from her magazine with a grin. "Really? Tell me!"

"It's in the city centre. A building that houses mostly legal firms. They are advertising for someone to open a café in the lobby."

"So we wouldn't have to pay goodwill."

"Exactly. We could start from scratch and have it exactly as we want."

"Perfect!"

"It would still cost lots to set up."

"I've got that money coming to me from the divorce, so it won't be a problem."

"Yeah, but I've gotta put some in. I think I'll hit my father up for some. Work on the guilt he feels for leaving me."

"We'll work out something, but we'll be partners, don't you worry."

"It'll be like the old days when we worked in the coffee-shop together with the Greek guy."

"Cheeky teenagers. We've changed a bit!"

"Speak for yourself." Raz said this with a twinkle in her eye.

In the next few weeks the two women went about the exhausting legal, financial, and physical work necessary to open a coffee shop. Julia watched Raz carefully to make sure her friend wasn't taking on too much, but they were exciting times, and Raz went from strength to strength.

Raz had begun seeing a psychologist. Julia could tell by the look on her friend's face when she finished each session that some hard truths had been unearthed, but didn't question Raz about them. She simply tried to provide her friend with the support needed to face these demons.

Raz's unit wasn't in a wonderful location and it was very small. Julia's bedroom, in particular, only had room for a single bed and a bedside table. There was nowhere to hang clothing. Occasionally she thought about moving out and finding her own place, but the thought of leaving Raz made her feel sad. So she stayed. At least she was saving money by being there.

After several months of working on the details, it was time for the fit-out of the coffee shop. Raz had the eye of an artist and designed a wonderful café that had the shop-fitter excited. This consisted of black ironwork with bronzed leaves, running like vines. The tables and chairs had the same matt-black metal finish and timber tops with a marine-standard varnish.

Although their coffee-making equipment would be state-of-the-art, they also found some antique machines for display. They hired a top-notch barista and a part-time waitress.

Raz and Julia were in the lobby of the building every day, ensuring the fit-out progressed to their satisfaction. Both noticed the interested looks of the men and women who passed them several times a day, and it wasn't just the coffee shop that was getting attention. There were a few men displaying interest in Julia and Raz as well.

They had already been warned about the slow-down between Christmas and into the first week of the

New Year, which was around when the café would be ready to open. They saw this as a positive, a chance to make sure the equipment worked satisfactorily and that everyone knew their roles. They set a date for the Grand Opening on the 8th January, but were operating a week prior to that.

They all wore black polo shirts and black pants. The shirts sported the café logo on the breast pocket and across the back. The aprons were also black with the logo of the upmarket coffee brand.

On 7th January, Julia treated herself and Raz to a series of beauty treatments, including hair and nails. On the 8th, they were at the café early, offering free coffee and treats to everybody who passed. Both the barista and waitress kept the coffee coming, while Julia and Raz mingled with the customers. It was a busy few hours, but they were able to find out a great deal about the law firms upstairs.

Julia became aware of one man in particular who seemed to spend a lot of time at her elbow. This situation had even caught the attention of Raz, who looked on in amusement. Later they would laugh about it.

"He seemed quite taken with you!" Raz's eyes were dancing.

"No, he was so old!"

"I'm sure you could have some fun with him, though."

"I don't think so. Who was he, anyway?"

"His name is Peter. Big wheeler dealer barrister, corporate law. That's where the big bucks are."

"Really? Well, I'm not interested."

"Keep an open mind. Could be fun!"

Costas's and Nicholas's eyes lit up when they saw the coffee machine, all stainless-steel with steam rising.

"Wow!" breathed Nicholas as he watched the barista make hot chocolates for each of them.

Julia led them to a table and told them to sit still while she brought over their drinks and some biscuits. She brought coffee for herself and sat down, smiling at her sons.

"So, what's new?"

"Dad's got a new girlfriend!" Costas wriggled in his seat.

"Really? How wonderful."

"And she's Greek!"

Julia was surprised that Costas would even understand the meaning of that statement, and realised he must have overheard conversations on the subject. "Is she nice?"

"Yeah. Cooks great food."

"And Dad makes goo goo eyes at her all the time," said Nicholas.

Julia laughed. "That's great news, boys. You make sure you're really nice to her. You want her to stay, right?"

Costas frowned. "We'd rather have you back, Mum."

"Of course you would, but you mustn't think that's going to happen."

"Never?"

"Never, so you'd better make sure Dad's girlfriend stays happy."

"Okay, Mum."

Raz walked over, wiping her hands on a cloth. "Hey boys."

"Hey Auntie Rachel," the boys chorused.

"How do you like the café?"

"Good!" the boys said at the same time.

"Did you know that Barry there is the best barista in Australia?"

"Really?" Nicholas was impressed. "But what's a barista?"

Raz smiled. "A person who makes coffee. With a machine like that."

"And he's the best in Australia? Wow." Raz ruffled his hair and moved away. "Is he really, Mum?"

"Oh, probably." Julia was already distracted. She was thinking about Barry and how much they were paying him. They had to sell a river of coffee and a mountain of cakes to even come close to breaking even. She shook herself and looked at the boys. "What do you want to do today?"

"What can we do?"

"Um, don't know. Movie? Or we could go to the museum and see the dinosaurs."

"Dinosaurs!" said the boys in unison.

"Okay. Finish your hot chocolates and we'll go."

CHAPTER TWENTY

Peter was frowning when Julia opened the door. "I thought I'd come to the wrong place. You live here?"

"Yes, Raz and I are sharing at the moment."

"Oh, I see." He looked over Julia's shoulder to the interior. "At least it doesn't look too bad inside."

"Yes, maybe we'll have a coffee here after the show, eh? We'd better get going."

Peter stood aside as Julia brushed past him. He opened the door to his Jaguar with a flourish. Julia laughed. "No need for a car. It's only a five minute walk."

Peter looked at her as though she were mad. "Walk? I've got a parking voucher." He looked into the sky as if hoping for a stray rain cloud.

"Yes, walk."

"All right then."

"It's the benefit of inner-city living."

"Hmm." Peter sounded unconvinced.

They walked companionably for a few minutes

before Julia spoke. "I heard a rumour about you the other day."

"Oh?"

"That you're married. Have been for more than thirty years."

Peter laughed. "Terrible lies."

"It's not true then?"

He sighed. "Well, yes. Guilty as charged."

"I see."

"But you still came out with me, even after hearing that?"

"I really wanted to see the show."

Peter threw his head back and roared with laughter. "Fair enough. Well said."

"See, there's the Cultural Centre already."

"Hmm. Will the Jag be safe in your street?"

"Oh, I think so. Nothing a good panel beater couldn't fix." She saw his face go pale and laughed. "Gotcha."

"Very funny."

Peter was attentive, bringing her a glass of champagne before lining up to buy programs. She watched him trying to make his way back to her, hindered by all the people stopping him to say hello.

Soon the bells were warning that the doors would be closing. They made their way to the best seats in the house. "This is lovely, thank you Peter."

"Only the best for you, my dear."

Raz's face wore the most shocked expression that Julia had ever seen.

"He's doing what?"

"Leaving his wife."

"To be with you?"

"Well...yes."

"And you want him to do that? You want to be with him?"

"Why not?"

"Gawd, Jules. He's so old!"

"But as he says, he's very low-mileage."

"You two have had sex. Right?"

"No."

"So how do you know if he's okay in the sack?"

Julia shrugged. "I'll worry about that later. I'm not making a commitment, you know. If it doesn't work out then I'll leave."

"After he's left his wife for you?"

"He's not leaving her for me. He's leaving her because he wants to. It was his idea. I have never asked him to do so. Never even suggested it."

"This'll cause some gossip around the coffee shop!"

Julia laughed without mirth. "Yeah, the top barrister in the top chambers leaving his wife for someone that serves coffee!"

"Don't let them make you feel like that."

"Can you imagine what that horrible Jones, head of chambers will say?"

"Ha! This will rock his little world, won't it?"

Julia chewed her lip. "You'll be happy for me, won't you?"

"Sure, honey. I hope you're not moving out straight away."

"Nope. He's going to find a place to live, then tell his wife."

"So we'll have a bit of time before the shit hits the fan."

"For sure. We'll have to pack some fun in—just the two of us—before that happens."

The line for service was ten deep. Raz was taking orders, Barry tapping and tamping and pouring, while Julia found the right customer to hand the coffee to.

"Damien? Ah, there you are. A skinny-cino just how you like it."

"Thank you, you gorgeous woman. When are you going to take me up on my offer? Very few women can resist me, you know."

Julia gave the young lawyer a playful smile. "I'm too old for the likes of you."

"I bet you could teach me a thing or two."

"Ha!" Julia went back to passing coffees around. Out of the corner of her eye, she saw Peter moving through the foyer towards the elevator. It was the first time she'd seen or heard from him in two days. He didn't look around at her, just gave a half wave as he passed through at a fast pace. She saw Raz raise her brows in surprise.

As the rush quietened, Raz went to one of the tables and wiped it down. She sat heavily and motioned to Julia to do the same. Julia didn't feel like talking, but did as her friend asked.

"Trouble in paradise?"

"Don't know." Julia swept the back of her hand across her forehead. "He was going to tell the wife the other night."

"That he was leaving?"

"Yes."

"And?"

"Silence. Haven't seen or heard from him since."

"What do you think it means?"

"Well, the obvious is that he has cold feet. But there have been other issues as well."

"Like what?"

"He assumed I was going to stop working here. He plans to retire soon and thought I'd be with him 24/7."

"Oh, dear."

"Other things as well. He met my boys." Julia looked down at her feet. "It didn't go well."

"Did they play up?"

"Sort of. Just normal boy stuff. We all went for a picnic—a drive in the mountains."

"I suppose they got bored."

"Yes, and I think they might have tuned in to my nervousness—you know?"

"Ah, yes."

"Then there's you."

"Me?"

"He thinks you're a bad influence."

Raz threw back her head and laughed. "Why?"

"Reckons you're a 'bit bohemian'."

"Is there anything about your life he likes?"

Julia sighed. "I think it's an age thing. He's set in his ways and doesn't like his carefully constructed world rocked, if you know what I mean."

"So what are you saying to him? I hope you're not going to let him walk all over you."

Julia's eyes filled with tears. "It's just hard."

"I bet it is. Do you still want to be with him?"

"Don't know. I don't even know where I stand at the moment." She pulled a tissue from a pocket and blew her nose.

"Bastard."

"No, he's not that. He's just a man who's used to getting his own way. He has a compliant wife, adoring daughters, and assistants in his workplace. Things are easy for him. Well they were until I came along."

"You're not going to try to contact him, are you?"

Julia pulled the mobile telephone from her apron and looked at it. "I sent him a text."

"No answer?"

"Nope."

"You won't send him another, will you?"

"You don't think I should?"

"Here's an idea. Think of someone like, um, Grace Kelly. In this situation she'd lift her chin and maintain a dignified silence."

"I prefer channeling someone feistier. Sophia Loren. She'd fight tooth-and-nail for her man."

Raz smiled, but it wasn't reflected in her eyes. "Well, it's your ballgame, honey. Just take it easy, though." She stopped and looked down at her hands. When she lifted her eyes, Julia could see moisture there. "Life wasn't so bad with just the two of us, was it?"

"That's the thing. We're so happy, you and me. We have fun together and if we feel like male company we can always get some. I don't know why I'm even considering being with Peter."

"Why are you then?"

"It's hard to explain. I feel an emotional investment. I keep wanting to move forward. Finish something I started, sort of." She blew her nose again. "I just can't seem to help myself."

Peter arrived at the restaurant in a blue linen shirt and chinos. A cashmere pullover was draped across his shoulders, the sleeves tied in a loose knot at his chest. He'd slicked back his grey hair and had his glasses in a breast pocket. He sat heavily, without giving Julia a kiss, and sighed.

"It's a lot harder than I thought. Bloody awful." He dabbed his forehead with a handkerchief.

"So, fill me in. What's been happening in the last couple of weeks? You were going to tell your wife..."

"Yes, I went home full of resolve. I began talking..."

"And?"

"Oh, I was mouthing drivel. Couldn't get to the point."

"An articulate barrister like yourself lost for words?"

"Hmm? Oh yes. Frightful situation."

"So?"

"My girls arrived unexpectedly. They walked in and realised something was wrong. My wife said, and I quote, "I think your father is trying to tell me he wants a divorce.""

"Oh no!"

"Three hysterical women!" Peter wiped his brow again. "I ended up ringing my daughters' husbands to come and take them away. But before they got there, the two of them forced me to promise I'd stay."

"I see." Julia began to feel something unexpected. A relief was washing over her. Her life could go back to being simple and uncomplicated. At the same time she felt sad and let down. A strange contradiction.

"But things have moved on since then." Peter smiled at the waiter who was displaying the wine label.

"In what way?"

Peter tasted the chardonnay and nodded to the waiter, who poured some for Julia.

"Oh, endless conversations. It's been tiring. I haven't been concentrating on work at all. Jones is most concerned."

"Do they know anything at work about what's been going on?"

"Probably. I suspect Sylvia has rung Jones. Those two are always in cahoots." He sliced a scallop and popped it into his mouth, groaning in appreciation.

Julia looked at the view across the river. The water was sparkling, and a tiny yacht was making its way upstream. She wished she were the person standing under the sails, relaxed and carefree. She wanted to stand and leave, tell Peter she was sick of all the nonsense, but seemed unable to do so.

"So?"

"Oh, well, I don't know what to tell you. Things are progressing, but there are good days and bad days. Sylvia keeps trying to tell me it's male menopause."

"I think you are too old for that."

Peter frowned. "Maybe, maybe not. She has a point. Look, the thing is this. I know how I want the rest of my life to look, and it doesn't include Sylvia."

Julia could feel irritation rising, and it was causing a pulsing in her temples. "Well then leave her or don't leave her. Or leave her for yourself, not to be with me. Leave her and live alone. Just do something!" She stopped, realising her voice had risen.

Peter looked around the restaurant and frowned. "No need for hysterics."

At that point Julia could have poked him in the eye with a fork. She took some deep breaths. "There. No hysterics."

"Good girl."

It was the condescending tone that was the last straw. She unfolded her legs and rose slowly from the chair. Lifting her nose like Grace Kelly would, she smiled confidently at the waiter as she strode out of the restaurant.

She'd show that bloody, pontificating bastard what she was made of.

During the following week Julia saw Peter's shadow from time to time, slipping through the foyer while looking the other way. The route past the coffee shop was the only entrance to the building, other than through the basement, so these attempts of his not to be noticed as he went to and from work, were causing Julia and Raz some hilarity.

Although she laughed with her friend, Julia was stressed and was having trouble sorting out her feelings. At times she felt her heart crumbling, while at other times she'd tell herself that it was over and that was for the good.

Raz watched her friend closely through this time, making sure she stayed busy. Occasionally Julia would feel Raz's eyes looking deeply into her own as though trying to fathom Julia's mental state.

One night, they were relaxing at home, listening to music while reading, when they heard a loud knocking. Raz went to the door and found Peter standing there holding a bunch of roses.

"Gee, for me, Peter? You shouldn't have."

Peter blinked and then a smirk crossed his face. "Is Julia in?"

"I don't know. I'll have to check. Are you in, Julia?"

There was silence for a moment. Julia sauntered to the door with attitude. "Oh, hello Peter."

The man was looking flustered. "Julia, I've come to talk. Good news."

"Oh?"

Peter looked at Raz. She took a step back from the door and leaned against the wall with folded arms. She lifted a brow.

Julia smiled. "Anything you can say to me can be said to Raz as well." She walked and stood next to her friend.

Peter looked from one to the other. He walked in and closed the door, then placed the roses on the dining table. Clearing his throat, he grabbed the lapel of his suit coat and began talking in a loud voice.

"Ladies and gentlemen of chambers." He lowered his voice and said, "This is the speech I have just given."

The girls nodded, enjoying the theatrics.

"I would like to make an announcement. It is with regret that Sylvia and I have decided to part after a period of more than thirty years. This has not been an easy decision, but I must assure you that she and I will remain good friends. She is the mother of my two beautiful daughters and has earned my respect for the way she has raised the family and managed our home." He took another breath. "Now, I know there are rumours circulating about a particular young lady whom most of you know. I would like to have it known that the dissolution of my marriage is in no way related to my friendship with this person. If I hear any rumours to the contrary, be aware that I will deal with these harshly." Peter winked at Julia who smiled in return. "I am aware that my personal affairs have been affecting my work. This is now over and I appreciate the efforts of those who have stepped up to help. From now on it will be business as usual. Thank you for your time."

"Wow." Julia's eyes were shining.

"What do you think, girls?" Peter looked pleased with himself.

Raz coughed. "Quite a performance, I must say. What will everyone think when Julia moves in with you?"

"The fuss will die down very quickly. There will be other issues to gossip about. We'll just wait until then."

Julia frowned. "So, I'm not moving in with you yet?"

"No, but we can still see each other, eh?"

"But it's not very romantic, is it?"

"Patience, dear girl. It's for the best."

Raz snorted and walked into her bedroom, closing the door with a bang.

CHAPTER TWENTY-ONE

Peter's new house was a testament to his good taste and love of fine things. It was a worker's cottage that had been extensively renovated and extended. Appearances were deceptive. From the road it looked well-kept but small. It wasn't until you entered that the full size of the house was revealed.

The rear deck faced northeast and was a delightful place to eat breakfast year-round, but particularly in spring when Brisbane displayed clear blue days. On this day, rainbow lorikeets were feeding on the nectar of a nearby tree, their flashes of colour delightful in the green canopy.

Julia was dressed in her gym outfit. She had spent the night at Peter's and would leave when her breakfast digested. Peter was wearing his customary dressing gown, which was burgundy with gold trim. Velour. He was reading the newspaper and commenting on news stories.

Julia sipped her orange juice and sighed. "Oh,

it's so nice here. What a beautiful outlook. So much nicer than Raz's place."

Peter peered at her over the top of the newspaper. "Yes, well we must get you out of that situation soon."

"That was always the plan."

"Hmm. She is a totally unsuitable companion for somebody like yourself, my dear. You have breeding and manners."

"But she's been my best friend since school."

"I know, but sometimes we outgrow people. I certainly have. If we don't move forward, we limit our own potential."

"How do you mean?"

"She is an unreliable business partner. You are better off cutting her loose."

Julia had to agree with Peter on that point. Raz *was* unreliable. She also had a habit of emptying the till from time to time and leaving a promissory note.

"That would certainly solve the problem of having to split the profits with her. The business isn't going well enough for two partners."

"Well, there you go. Come to some settlement with her. Our firm can handle the legals gratis, you'll just need to pay costs."

"But how can I buy her out? Money-wise that is."

Peter frowned over his newspaper. "I thought you had a good divorce settlement. I understood your former husband was a wealthy man."

"I didn't get a large settlement."

"Why not, my love?"

"I didn't want one. Didn't seem fair."

"Good heavens! Silly girl! What did you do?"

Julia lifted her nose. "I just took enough to set

up the coffee shop and to live on for a while. Oh, and a car."

"That was it?"

"Yes, well he was keeping the boys and paying for their education. He had built the business from scratch, a long time before I knew him. It wasn't fair to go for a 50/50 settlement."

Peter shook his head. "You should have got someone in our firm to handle it. We have two excellent divorce lawyers. You could have been set up for life."

"I didn't want to. Let's forget about that now. We're talking about me buying Raz out."

"Or even better, she could buy your share."

"Then how would I support myself?"

"You could move in here. I'd support you."

This reminded Julia of the negotiations for the adoption of her baby—the system of manners used. There were no ultimatums. No raised voices. At the same time, each party knew what was on the table and what was at stake.

Julia had been waiting to move in with Peter since he left his wife two years before. The invitation had never been issued. On occasion he'd just make reference to, 'when the time was right'. Now Julia understood the rules. If she sold her share of the coffee shop, she could move in.

"So, what if I bought Raz's share?"

Peter flicked his paper. "I suppose you could still move in."

"And where would I get the funding?"

"A bank loan could be arranged. I have contacts."

So he wouldn't go so far as to loan her the money. Their finances would remain separate. This was to be the way of it.

Julia realised she was being manipulated, knew she should rebel, but reasoned that once they were living together as de facto man and wife that things would change. They would throw their lot in together. Move forward as a couple. The situation would definitely improve.

Raz seemed unsurprised when Julia made the buyout offer, and accepted almost angrily. The deal moved forward swiftly.

One day in late spring, Julia packed her meagre belongings and went to find Raz to say goodbye. She searched inside and out and up the street, but her friend was unusually absent. Julia left the key on the dining table and closed the door behind her. It seemed like the end of an era.

"I just don't get you!" Raz screamed at her. "You're pushing me away, and you're so damned cold about it. But then you are such a cold bitch. You always have been. I think about how easily you walked away from your little baby. You haven't hardly mentioned her since. I reckon you don't give her a thought—just considered yourself lucky to get away scot-free."

Julia was wide-eyed with shock. She and Raz's little get-together had gone seriously wrong. "How dare you bring Emilie into this? You've got no goddamned idea of what it's been like." She stood, clenching and unclenching her fists. "I've had to live with the shame of having an illegitimate child, as well as missing her every single day of my life. Every day I wake and wonder about her. When Camille sends the updates it's like...like I'm being eaten alive from the inside, but I can't tell her to stop writing. So don't you sit there all self-righteous and accuse me of being cold about

Emilie. Just because I haven't mentioned it to you..."

Julia had seen she'd hit a nerve with Raz, that her friend was regretting the harsh words. She knew that these words had come from a bad place, that place of rejection that Raz was always so afraid of.

It suited Julia to stay angry, however. The time had come to take a break from her friend, and this made it easier. Raz tried several times to apologise, leaving muffled messages on Julia's mobile, but they went unanswered.

As time passed, however, Julia was forced to recognise some hard truths. Peter was a cold man who would never fully embrace a life with her. He would attend family events without her and without apology. He kept his possessions and money separate to hers. He seemed disinclined to fully immerse himself into the relationship.

Julia came to realise that she had sacrificed the best part of her life for a man who would never fully welcome her in to his.

PART THREE

CHAPTER TWENTY-TWO

Julia wouldn't let go of Raz's hand as she rummaged in her handbag for the front door keys and undid the complicated set of locks. She threw her belongings on the floor and pulled her friend to the sofa.

"Did my brother contact you? What did he say? Oh, God, I'm so glad you're here. Will you ever forgive me?"

Raz still looked half-asleep. She smiled at the other woman's ramblings. "Yes, Christopher rang me. He said you were up to your normal tricks, running away from home and keeping secrets from everyone, including him. Yes, I forgive you as you knew I would. Besides, I said some nasty things back then."

"Oh, thank you. You have no idea..."

"You look like shit. You've lost weight. Why?"

"Lots of reasons. There's been a lot happening." She looked into Raz's face and smiled. "Oh, God. I can't believe you're here."

Raz rose to her feet and went to the kitchen.

Julia could hear the kettle being turned on and cups rattling. Raz's voice could be heard over the noise. "Keep talking. I can hear."

Julia joined her friend in the kitchen. "You know Peter has had a massive heart attack."

"Christopher told me."

"He was alone because I went away."

"I can't say I blame you for leaving—"

"No, it wasn't like that. Well, it wasn't hard to go, but there were other reasons."

"Like what?"

"She got in touch with me, Raz. My daughter. From France."

Raz's hands became still. "Really? What did you do?"

"Nothing at first. She wrote a letter and I read it and put it in a drawer."

"I see."

"But then, well, a lot of stuff happened. I began feeling bad, physically I mean. No energy. I was dropping things. Sometimes I had difficulty swallowing."

"What was causing it?"

"Peter said it was overwork. Said I had to sell the coffee shop and relax more. We could spend more time together."

"So he was still singing that old tune. I guess you haven't changed your mind about that."

Julia gave Raz a level look. "What do you reckon?"

"I dunno. Haven't been around to see how you two have been getting along."

"Let's just say that the thought of being around him 24/7 wasn't an attractive one."

"I get it. So what happened next?"

"I didn't think it was caused by overwork. Stress maybe. I went to the doctor. He said he wanted to rule out a couple of things—referred me to a specialist."

"Like what sort of things?"

"Those symptoms are fairly broad and could be caused by many conditions. He suggested that the specialist check for Multiple Sclerosis."

"Whoa! But you don't have it, right?"

"I went to the specialist. He agreed with my GP, and said that they should investigate further. There was a whole list of tests that had to be done." Julia slid to the kitchen floor. "Test after test after test."

"I get it. Lots of tests. What about the results?"

"Don't know. I went through them all—MRI, lumbar puncture, blood tests and more. After each test I'd have to return to the specialist for him to check the results. Then he'd decide what had to be done next. It was time consuming and expensive. Finally they ruled out Multiple Sclerosis and some other conditions."

"Glad to hear that."

"Yes, well that sounds like good news, but then the specialist said he had to investigate further. There are other conditions. Motor Neurone, for example."

"So you had more tests—"

"Couldn't."

"Couldn't what?"

"Face them. I had the overwhelming desire to see my daughter. She has her own little girl now, Isabel. I had to go to France."

"What did old poo-face say about that?"

"I organised it before I told him. I wasn't going to ask if that was all right because I figured he'd say no, or he'd want to go with me."

"But you needed to do this alone."

"Absolutely. I responded to Emilie's letter, via

email so it was quicker. I also emailed her parents. I booked flights. Then I told Peter."

"So he knew about Emilie?"

"Not until then. He was angry that I'd hidden that part of my life from him. I haven't told him about my illness yet, either. Not until I have concrete results."

Raz laughed. "You should have told him not to feel too bad. You do that to everyone."

"Very funny. Anyway, his being angry made the whole thing easier. I simply left on my own."

"Okay, so let's backtrack a bit. You didn't have the new tests. When will you?"

"The neurologist told me to contact him as soon as I got back. If I still had the same symptoms after a holiday, he'd re-assess my condition and then I'd undergo the tests. Motor Neurone Disease is considered a very difficult condition to diagnose correctly."

"What tests?"

"Something called 'nerve conductor studies'. Another called electromyography. More blood tests. Another MRI scan..."

"Jeez."

"But it could be nothing. Or it could be stress. The symptoms didn't seem quite as bad while I was away." Julia looked at the ceiling. "Who knows?"

"So tell me what happened in France."

Julia raised herself from the kitchen floor. "Let's have our cuppa in the lounge where it's comfortable. I'll tell you there.

Julia enjoyed sharing stories of her trip to France with Raz, mostly because her friend had been to many of the places, and knew some of the people. Their shared history made the telling enjoyable.

"The chateau was almost exactly as we left it. Remember how Pierre was adamant that it was preserved exactly as it should be? I reckon every blade of grass was still the same. Pierre had aged, though. Naturally. Wider and grey-haired."

Raz wiggled in her seat in excitement. "And his wife—what was her name again?"

"Camille. She'd aged better because she was never a great beauty. Her attraction came from inside. She still had that. Both of them were as gracious and kind as ever."

Julia went on to describe arriving at the chateau and being welcomed like an old friend. She expected some reserve from Emilie's adoptive parents, but there was none. It was written in the contract, after all, that if Julia ever wanted to meet Emilie, it would be permitted. This was achieved with no angst, although Julia still worried that they were hiding misgivings behind a polite facade. She knew that if she were in their place, she'd be a mess.

What helped was that Emilie had instigated contact, not Julia. Her adoptive parents had supported the idea. This made Julia feel less uncomfortable.

She stayed a week in Pierre and Camille's home, spending it mostly with Emilie and Isabel. Emilie's husband, Guy, joined them when he could, but as chief winemaker, was kept busy.

Emilie herself was a Master of Wine. She and Guy had met while studying for this qualification, a process that took three years. It was rare for a winery to employ one Master of Wine, but in the case of Pierre and Camille's vineyard, they could proudly claim two.

The family owned a holiday home on the coast, in the Brittany region. One morning, Julia, Emilie, and

Isabel joined a convoy that drove to this 'cottage' that was, in fact, a very large house. There were three vehicles in the procession, including a van which was full of supplies for a week, as well as another that carried three servants. Guy would come later in the week to spend a night or two.

Emilie had warned Julia about the lack of mobile telephone reception at the cottage. This didn't concern Julia, who was thankful that Peter's calls, always full of complaints about being left alone, would no longer be possible.

It was a perfect week, both weather-wise and for the bond that grew between the three generations. They didn't need to move from the cottage, as the servants provided everything they needed. It was a wonderful rest.

Emilie, aware of Julia's health concerns, had suggested some changes to her diet and general health regime. The two of them practised yoga and meditation. They drank only water and vegetable juices. At mealtimes they ate raw foods. They went for walks along the beach, kilometre after kilometre, at sunrise and sunset. Julia felt enormous benefits after only the one week.

"But," Julia said, "the week ended, and we began the drive back to the chateau. As the mobile went back into range, I found the world had gone mad. There was message after message about Peter, from his daughters, my sons, George, my parents, Christopher, the hospital—it was crazy."

"So you decided to turn the car around and go back to the cottage in Brittany and let everything sort itself out?"

Julia laughed. "Oh, you're funny! I wish I had now."

Raz smiled. "So it's all pretty bad."

"That's not all. Barry, who was meant to manage the coffee shop while I was away, took off and left me in the lurch. Becki and Trudy found another guy, Steven, who seems okay, but now there's a rent review coming up."

"And business hasn't been any good since you bought me out, hey?"

"Well, the GFC hit me really badly for a while, and I've got to pay interest on the bank loan I took to pay you out."

Raz nodded. "What can I do right now to help?"

"Just be here. I feel so much better now, since you arrived. How did you come so quickly? Don't you have a job?"

"Nah. I made a lot of money years ago on dotcom start-ups. I've been making good money since with other investments. It leaves me free to do some writing, screenplays mostly."

"Wow. You're so damned clever. I'm glad to see you putting it to good use. Do you have a man in your life?"

"Ditched the last one a week ago. Miserable bastard. Enough about me, tell me something I can help with, practically."

"Work in the café? Wave a magic wand? Fix my health? Make all my other problems go away?"

Raz laughed and snapped her fingers. "Consider it done."

By the time the women slowed down their intense conversation, it was nearly nine o'clock. Neither of them had eaten much all day. While Julia went to the bathroom, Raz began rummaging through the refrigerator. "Jeez, Jules. All you have in here are vegetables."

Julia joined Raz in the kitchen. "Yeah, sorry. Special diet. I've been trying to eat healthily, like in Brittany."

"Ah, I get it. Do you juice the vegetables?"

"Yeah, for breakfast and lunch. Cook them for dinner, and you know how much I hate vegetables!"

"How about rice?"

"Organic brown rice is okay. There's some in the cupboard."

"How about I make us some stir-fried veggies with brown rice then?"

"That would be great, thanks. I'll make up a bed for you and set the table."

The women went about their jobs until Raz called out to Julia that the dinner was ready. As Raz put the plates on the table, she asked about wine.

"I'm still not drinking, sorry."

"Bummer."

"You can have some. Peter will have red somewhere."

"Nah. Do me good to go without." They began eating. "So you never ended up marrying him, eh?"

Julia had a mouthful of food. She swallowed but began choking. Raz thumped her on the back until it stopped. "Sorry, great stir fry, but sometimes I have problems swallowing. He never got a divorce."

"Really? How long has it been since he left her?"

"Nine years. Nearly ten."

"That's strange. And the wife has never started the divorce proceedings?"

"Nope." Julia went on to tell Raz how the wife and daughters sat by Peter's sickbed 24/7 and tried to leave her in the cold. Raz laughed until her sides ached.

"How do you feel about that?"

Julia shrugged. "Leaves me free to sort out all this other mess."

"Would you have married him if he did get divorced?"

"I don't know. The thing is—well he's just a one trick pony."

"A what?"

"A one-trick pony. All he did was change where he lives. He did nothing else. I'm not mentioned in his will. We have no joint bank accounts. He doesn't like or show any interest in my children. He's never shown me much love, let alone affection."

"I thought that might be the case."

"Do you know that if there are family celebrations, with his daughters, he is happy for them to exclude me from invitations? He just goes alone."

"That is really low."

"He likes to be seen in public with me on his arm—that makes him happy. It's like he wanted a younger life companion and got himself one and that's it."

"And the sex?"

"Not bad. Not wonderful. When he stopped making me feel so special—when I realised I wasn't number one in his life—that affected the way I felt about him sexually. I needed him to be in my corner. Every woman needs a champion, someone who will fight for her—who will tell anyone who is treating her badly to piss off. He never did that. He allowed his daughters to be rude and ignore me. As soon as I realised that this was going to be the situation in the future, I found I didn't want to please him anymore. In any case, I'm sure sex will be almost non-existent after this heart attack."

"So, why haven't you left this arsehole? You're still an attractive woman, you know."

Julia shrugged. "I thought about it often. Then I began to feel sick. I'll show you something." She went into the study and came out with Peter's notepad, where "Fix living arrangements" was scrawled across the page. "I think he'd come to his own conclusion that we should part."

"And I suppose you'll be expected to nurse him when he comes home. How do you feel about that?"

"How do you reckon I feel? After a few days of that I'll feel like smothering him with a pillow, or leaping off the highest building. If I'm going to degenerate with MND, I don't want to be spending the balance of my life nursing a sick old man."

Raz ate silently for a moment. Julia could almost see the wheels turning in her friend's mind.

"But the wife—the one he's still married to—"

"Yeah."

"I bet she'd love to nurse him."

Julia looked at Raz with a slow smile. "She and the daughters would be very happy to do so."

"They would think they'd won a victory against you."

"When all the time they'd be doing me the biggest favour."

"You couldn't let them know that."

"Oh, no. But how could we pull this one off?"

"Leave it to your old mate Raz, darling. Leave it to me."

Julia and Raz went to the coffee-shop early to begin

setting up. Raz began taking the chairs and tables out of storage while Julia set up the cups, saucers and coffee-machine. She reached under the counter and pulled out a plastic bag. "Here!" She threw it at Raz.

"What is it?"

"The new uniform. Try it on."

While Raz went to the bathroom to change, Julia saw Steve walking through the main doors. She liked the way he moved, like a big cat. "Hey Steve."

"Hi Julia."

"You'll be glad to know I've found you a helper."

"Wow. You're the greatest. Who is it?"

Just then Raz walked into the lobby, tying the apron around her waist. Steve raised his brows. "Whoa. Nice."

Julia looked at him in surprise and swung around to view what he could see. Raz with her multi-coloured hair and strange jewellery. Androgynous body. At least ten years older than him.

"Hey, come and meet our new barista. This is Steve."

Raz looked up and straight into Steve's eyes. Hers crinkled at the edges to match his. There was silence for several heartbeats. Steve held out his hand to Raz, and she placed her tiny one into it. He covered hers with his left hand and nodded as though answering a question. She nodded too.

Julia was watching this with fascination, but people were beginning to flood into the lobby. Becki raced in and began sorting things behind the counter. "Okay, folks. It's show time!" said Julia. Raz and Steve shook their heads as though recovering from a long sleep and propelled themselves into action. "Rachel and I will be here through the first rush, and should be back for the second one. Other than that we have stuff to do. Okay?"

"Brilliant!" said Steve with shining eyes.

CHAPTER TWENTY-THREE

"Rachel, is that you?" Amanda's face was beaming as she saw her two school friends walking into the ward together.

"Hey, Amanda. Julia said you were working here. How are you?"

"Great. You're looking good."

Julia peered into the ICU. "Are they here?"

"Of course. Go into the waiting room and I'll shoo them out."

Julia squeezed Amanda's arm. "You're such a pal. Thanks."

"Not a problem."

Julia and Amanda walked away, but when Julia went into the waiting room, Raz waited in the corridor. She pretended to look out the window while the mother and two daughters huffed out of the unit and along the hallway.

"It's not fair, Mum. How can they treat you like that?" This was the plump daughter with the bad skin.

Sylvia was buxom, with hair dyed black like a tar-covered helmet. "Well, I guess she should be allowed to visit him. Sometimes." The three of them faded into the distance.

Amanda made a sign from the nurses' station and Raz told Julia the coast was clear. They went in to Peter's bedside. To Julia, he seemed totally unchanged. She took his cold hand and rubbed the fingers.

Raz took Amanda aside. Julia could hear her two friends talking in the distance. Raz was asking a lot of questions about Peter's condition. After five minutes she reappeared by Julia's side, seeming satisfied.

"So what do you do here? I mean, you can't do anything." Raz was looking about her, tapping her foot. "This place gives me the creeps."

"Yes, but I have to stay for a little while."

"I suppose so." Raz went to the end of the bed and looked at the chart. "Holy moly, he's on some drugs!"

"I bet he is."

"You should see this list!"

"I can never read it."

Amanda returned from talking to the relatives of another patient. "So, anything else new?"

Raz shook her head. "Hey, but we should get together—the three of us—like old times. Why don't you come to the coffee shop when you knock off?"

"Yeah, I finish at two. Where is it?"

They told her, and she wrote down the address. "Great. See you then!"

Julia and Raz walked out with a sense of relief. It was like leaving prison. "But," said Raz with a grin. "We've now got an ally on the inside."

Amanda arrived at the coffee-shop before three o'clock. Raz saw her first, giving a bright greeting and seating her at a table removed slightly from the others. Amanda was then treated with pastries and coffee. The three of them reminisced about school days and getting into trouble.

"You two were the mischief makers. I was a good girl." Amanda smiled fondly.

"Yeah, but we tried to lead you astray!"

"True, Rachel. Looking back, I can't work out why I didn't let my hair down a bit."

"It's easy to see that now with the shadow of middle age starting to cast a pall..." Raz looked mischievous.

Julia laughed. "That's today's happy thought."

Amanda didn't seem keen to leave at closing time. She suggested they move on to a bar which was located a block away. Raz winked at Julia and agreed quickly.

For the next few hours the bond between the three women was reignited by the sharing of confidences. Raz insisted that Julia tell Amanda about her health concerns. Julia felt self-conscious about this, but Amanda was a good listener. "That's why I'm only drinking soda water," said Julia. "I'm trying to be the healthiest I can possibly be."

Raz interrupted. "That's why I'm so glad you're working on Peter's ward. It has really helped Julia."

Amanda nodded. "Yeah, it's been a tough time. Glad to help. But jeez, Motor Neurone." She took Julia's hand. "I hope the tests come back negative."

"What really worries me," said Raz, "Is what will happen when Peter is released. She's not up to nursing him."

Amanda frowned. "Clearly not. Round-the-clock nursing is way too costly, too." The three women fell silent.

Raz tapped the table top. "You know, it's his ex-wife and daughters who are spending all his money. That's why he doesn't have enough for private nurses. I reckon they should be the ones to nurse him!" She said this as though the thought had only just occurred to her. "That Sylvia is still his wife, after all."

Amanda nodded, but didn't say anything. Raz looked at her watch and slid off the bar stool. "I've got a hot date tonight!"

Julia looked at her with a knowing smile. "Steve?"

"Indeed. We're off to see a band play. One of his Irish mates is in it."

Amanda collected her handbag and stood as well. "Is that the nice barista?"

"Yep. He and I have sort of clicked."

"Fantastic. Good luck." Amanda kissed each of her friends on the cheek. "I guess I'll be seeing you at the hospital."

"Oh, I meant to ask you—" Raz stopped and turned. "What are your hours in the ICU?"

Amanda squeezed her eyes shut. "Um, let me think. Oh yes!" She rattled off the details of her roster for the next seven days.

"Great. We'll see you then."

Julia was still awake when she heard Raz's key in the door. She called out, asking how the night went.

Raz stood in the doorway to Julia's bedroom with a lazy smile on her face. "Brilliant. Great music, great company."

"I thought you might not come home tonight."

"Yeah, me too. But I had a thought. It hit me like a bolt of lightning."

"Wow. What was it?"

"I felt that he and I should take our time. Get to know each other first."

"That's a new one for you."

"Yeah, strange isn't it? He's different. I get the sense that we've got a long time, that the story of us—the Rachel and Steve story—will unfold slowly. Like a rose blossoming on a time lapse movie."

"He's made you poetic."

Raz smiled and yawned. "Must get my beauty sleep. Hey, we're going to see the centre managers tomorrow—Steve and me."

"Oh, wow. Thank you. What do you think will happen?"

"Steve's been working hard on the figures. He can prove there has been a downturn in business since the GFC and that the café is only just beginning to recover. He's going for a rent reduction."

"Does he think he'll get it?"

"No, but they'll probably leave the rent as is."

"That would be a relief anyway."

Rachel waved airily. "Night, Jules. Sleep tight."

"You too, Raz. Dream of your lovely Irishman."

CHAPTER TWENTY-FOUR

Julia and Becki worked hard to cover for Steve and Raz, who were meeting the centre managers. "Here they are," said Becki as she caught sight of Raz's colourful hair. Julia saw the triumphant smiles on their faces, and knew the news would be good.

They stood before her like excited children. "Tell her!" said Raz, nudging the barista.

"You tell her."

"A ten-percent reduction!"

Julia's mouth fell open. "No! Really?"

"Really. You should have seen Steve. I was so proud of him."

"I bet. That's amazing. I swear you two are angels sent to look after me."

"Of course." Raz couldn't stop smiling.

The small team worked hard for the next few hours. At some point, Julia became aware of her mobile phone vibrating. It was a reminder to call the neurologist. She really needed to get that appointment.

How could she get past the unhelpful receptionist?

Julia caught the elevator to the next floor where there was a quiet area overlooking the river. She loved this place, a little-known refuge. There was plush carpet that absorbed noise, and windows constructed from huge panes of glass that always seemed magically clean.

There were two seats, both low and backless. She chose the one to the right, and lowered herself slowly, watching her breathing. For a few moments she sat silently, finding a place within her that was centered and peaceful. Her eyes were not quite closed, so that she was aware, but not fully.

Once she felt ready, she dialed the specialist's number. She smiled when she heard the familiar voice of the original receptionist she'd dealt with when she had made the first appointment.

"Oh, thank heavens. You're back."

There was laughter at the other end. "Gosh, I've heard that a lot since Monday when I came back from leave. Who's speaking?"

"Sorry. It's Julia. Julia Hawke."

The receptionist's voice changed tone, became serious. "Oh, Julia. I've been wondering how you are."

"I feel alright, but I was meant to see Dr. Cavendish when I got back from overseas, but the bloody bitch receptionist wouldn't give me an appointment for six weeks."

"Yes, I've heard all about her. Listen, I'd make a special appointment for you tonight—his last one for the day. I can see from your file it will just be a quick assessment before sending you for the tests. Five-thirty okay?"

"Absolutely. I'll see you then. Thanks so much."

It was with trepidation, therefore, that Julia kept

her appointment later that day. The neurologist asked another series of questions and printed some forms which he then signed and handed to her. "This is for your new MRI, to see if there have been changes since your first one. Also some blood tests. Make another appointment for late next week. If you have the tests done by this Friday, I'll have the results by then. Okay?"

Julia nodded numbly. She slept badly that night, worried about her future. After the morning rush in the coffee shop, she returned to the peaceful place on the first floor and made a call to schedule the tests. There was no feeling of satisfaction when this task was completed, just a heaviness of spirit.

She knew that she should work on her attitude—try to find some positives in the whole situation—but her loathing of all medical procedures was intense. She wished that the next week or so would just disappear.

Raz took an apple from the pile Julia was using in the vitamiser and bit into it loudly. "So the new rounds of tests—what's next."

"Another MRI and more blood tests. The specialist will then decide what's next when he sees the results."

"Ah. So, say they find it is Motor Neurone Disease. What then? How do they fix it?"

Julia looked at Raz levelly. "There's no cure."

"Huh? You're kidding me."

"No. There are drugs which help treat some forms of it."

"But they won't fix it?"

"No. It's all about slowing down its progression."

"Jeez, Jules. I thought they could fix just about

anything these days."

"Apparently not."

Raz looked at the apple in her hand and threw it in the bin. "Not hungry now. This is just too shitty."

"Nobody has said I have it yet."

"Yeah, and that's the thing. I don't think you have it."

"Great. I can stop worrying then."

"No, I'm serious. I mean, you can't. Look at you. You have such a strong life force."

"I don't feel it right now."

"Besides, you can't leave me."

"It wouldn't happen right away. It's degenerative. Look at Steven Hawking. He was diagnosed at twenty-one and is still alive at seventy."

"I don't know why that doesn't make me feel better." Raz picked at a ragged cuticle. "I always get in trouble when you're not around."

"You did a lot better last time. When I was with Peter."

"That's what you think." Raz looked at the floor. "Fortunately I had that good therapist."

Julia turned back to her friend and hugged her. "I'm not going anywhere right now. We should all just live one day at a time, moment to moment like the Buddhists say. Just now, at this very moment, you and I are together and happy. Let's just enjoy it."

"Lie still now, Ms. Hawke. Still like a statue. That's it."

Julia felt claustrophobic in the machine, hated every moment of the test. She took her mind back to the chateau in France and wandered through the fields surrounding it. She didn't know how long she spent doing this, but soon the platform she was lying on came free from the machine.

"Very good. You're done, Ms. Hawke." Julia could see the operator through the window to the next room. His voice sounded disembodied over the speaker.

"Are you sending the results straight to the specialist?"

"Yes, he'll have them by Monday."

"How do they look?"

The man shook his head. "You know I can't answer that."

"You can't blame a girl for trying."

She dressed and left the building quickly, happy to be in the open air. There was a park in the next block, and she walked to it, feeling light on her feet. The day was warm, and she peeled her cardigan from her arms. She lay it on the ground and then lowered herself until she was seated. The grass was cool and sweet under the giant trees.

What should she do now? It was Friday. Nicholas was due for dinner the next night, but they were having pizza, or at least Nicholas was. Nothing to do to prepare for that. She could go back to the coffee shop, but they didn't really need her. Peter. Should she go and see him? No, she didn't want to be in that ICU, so close to dying people on such a glorious day. She felt like celebrating life for as long as she had it.

The appointment with the specialist was scheduled for the following Thursday. After that more tests and another appointment. At that point, as soon as she knew the bigger picture, she'd have to start telling people. She'd consult with George about what she should tell the boys. Then there were her parents and Christopher. It was the thought of her brother more than anyone else that made her sad. She wondered how his court case was going, wondered if Damien would tell her if she asked.

A cloud slid across the sun, and to Julia the suddenly darker sky felt menacing. She shivered and moved to put her cardigan back on. Then she walked back to her car.

CHAPTER TWENTY-FIVE

The day dawned bright. On a whim, Julia went for an early walk in the gentle sunshine. There were two parks close to the house, and on this day she walked through one and then crossed a road to get to the second. She walked quickly, pumping her arms as she did so. It felt good.

Another walker came toward her from the opposite direction. Julia smiled and wished her a good morning. It *was* good, just at that moment.

She was relaxed. No more test for now. The MRI and blood test results had led to the specialist ordering further investigations. It had been a rough two weeks, but Julia had managed to remain calm. Her next appointment with the neurologist was later in the week, and she expected him to be able to tell her something concrete at that point.

Back at the house she noted that Raz's bed was still made-up. Julia smiled. Her friend deserved some happiness.

She began pulling fruit and vegetables from the refrigerator and preparing them for the vitamiser. She washed them carefully, trying to avoid chemicals, and vowed to find a supplier of good quality organic produce.

Nicholas's year twelve school photograph, the one he gave her on Saturday night, was on the refrigerator. Julia stared at it for a moment, happy at seeing her son standing tall and smiling among his school mates. She'd enjoyed his company, loved watching the enthusiasm shine on his face when he spoke about things he was passionate about. It didn't matter that she didn't share his enthusiasm for these subjects; he just loved telling her. This was in pleasant contrast to Costas, who had ceased communicating with her at any deep level from the age of fourteen.

She ran the vitamiser and poured the result into a tall glass. It was thick and green. She'd never gotten used to the taste, but masked it with apple juice.

Coronation Drive wasn't as busy as it normally was, and she reached her destination within fifteen minutes. Jim was waiting with a smile to guide her into the best car park. "What's the gossip, Jimmy?"

"Aw, nothin' much, Julia. It was a quiet weekend for me. The wife's been sick."

"Nothing serious I hope?"

"We 'ope not. Goin' to the quack's today for a check-up."

"Give her my best wishes." Julia threw him the keys and caught the elevator to the lobby.

She had just begun setting up when Steve and Raz walked through the big doors. They were holding hands, and there was a special glow emanating from them. Julia watched, feeling enjoyment at witnessing such happiness.

Raz caught sight of her and waved. "Hey Jules. Don't lift the tables—we'll take care of them."

"Thanks." Julia moved to behind the counter and began setting up. Becki ran in, breathless and red-faced, and began removing covers and wiping counters.

Raz sidled up to Julia. "Hey, I saw Amanda over the weekend."

"Great. I must call in at the hospital."

"Something might happen this week."

"Like what?"

"Like a plan I've been working on. Stay tuned." Raz smiled wickedly, winked, and walked away. Julia shook her head and began placing coins into the cash register. A flash of colour caught her eye. It was to her left, and when she turned to look, saw it belonged to a girl with vivid red hair who was wearing a green dress.

She was walking toward the coffee shop. The notable thing about this girl, other than the fact she was colourful, was the special smile on her face. Julia realised with a lurch of her stomach that the smile was aimed at Steve. He was filling the coffee machine and was oblivious to her approach. Julia could see Raz looking at the girl with a frown.

"Surprise!" the girl squealed.

Steve looked around and his mouth fell open. "What are ya doing here?"

"Missed ya, I did. Got a cheap fare. Have ya missed me?"

Raz and Julia were now both looking at Steve and the girl with mounting emotion. Julia was praying that the girl was a sister or other relation.

"Yeah, of course. When did you arrive?"

"At five thirty this morning."

"You'll need a coffee, then. Sit down and I'll

bring one over. I won't be able to talk for a while. It's our busy time."

The girl nodded and stood looking out the window. Julia noted her lovely skin, untouched by Australian sun. Her Irish accent, like Steve's, was musical. Julia looked at Raz who had lost the happy glow. She was biting her lip and holding back tears.

Julia sidled up to Steve. "Who's the little Irish girl then Steve?"

The barista didn't raise his head from the machine. "Oh, just a lass I knew in Ireland."

"Is she a girlfriend, by chance?"

"Um, she might think she is."

"Hmm. Could be problems brewing then."

"I'll sort it later."

"Okay."

As the customers began streaming toward them, desperate for their first coffees of the day, Julia hoped that Steve would 'sort it' sooner rather than later.

Close to lunchtime, Julia's mobile telephone rang.

"Hi Julia. It's Gail from Dr. Cavendish's rooms."

"Hi Gail. What's up?"

"Listen, I know your appointment is for Thursday, but Doctor wondered if you could make it today."

"Sure, but why?"

"He got the results of your tests and has shown them to a visiting specialist from Harvard Medical. He wants you to come in before the visitor flies out tomorrow."

"Alright. How about three thirty?"

"Four would be better. Is that okay?"

"Sure. See you then."

Julia terminated the call with a heavy heart. It would have been nicer to live in ignorance for a few more days.

When she turned back to the café, Steve was in a huddle with the Irish lass, and Raz was nowhere to be seen. "Where is Rachel, Becki?"

"Dunno. Turned and she'd gone."

"Steve?"

"Didn't see her go."

The afternoon hours crawled by. Julia was watching the clock for her appointment, while worrying about Raz. It wasn't like her friend to go off without telling her.

As the afternoon rush was fading, Julia's mobile telephone rang again. It wasn't a number she knew.

"Is that Julia?" The voice was harsh, loud and brittle.

"Yes. Who is this?"

"Sylvia. Sylvia Howard."

"Oh," said Julia weakly. What had happened?

"The nurse said she'd ring you, but I decided to get in first. Tell you the rules so there is no misunderstanding."

"What are you talking about?"

"Peter regained consciousness last night. Just briefly."

"Oh, that's good!"

"He only said a few words. We weren't there— he said it to the ward sister."

"Oh yes?"

"Said he wanted me there. Wanted me to take care of him from now on."

"What?"

"You heard me. He doesn't want you. He wants his true family looking after him."

"Which ward sister was this?"

"Oh, you don't believe me? You want to question her? Well she'll be ringing you soon. Don't try to fight it."

Julia could already hear another call coming through. Sylvia said a brusque goodbye and hung up. Julia took the next call.

"Jules, it's Amanda."

"Oh hi. I've just had Sylvia on the phone."

"Silly old bat. I told her to wait until I called you first."

"That was some news she had."

"Yes. Quite." Amanda fell silent. Julia got the message. Raz had pulled strings yet again.

"Well, we'd better let her have her way, hey? Keep the peace and all that."

Amanda chuckled. "Yep. Sounds like the way to go."

"I'll buy you a good bottle of French bubbles for that."

"No need, I didn't do anything."

"Regardless. I'll see you soon. Thanks."

Another problem solved.

But where was Raz?

Julia left early for her doctor's appointment, wanting to drive past some of Raz's favourite places on the way. Steve wouldn't know about the abandonment issues that Raz suffered from, about how fragile she could be underneath the brash, smart exterior.

Julia glided slowly past several places that Raz frequented, but there was no sign of the colourful hair. Julia looked at her watch and swung the car around. She drove to Wickham Terrace and found a space in the multi-storey parking lot. The minutes she had to wait for the green walk sign seemed like eons.

Gail smiled when she saw Julia. "They're almost ready for you. Take a seat."

The waiting room was deserted. Julia began deleting messages from her mobile telephone for something to do. A door opened and the neurologist motioned her in with a smile.

"Julia, meet my colleague, Dr. Meyers. He's been visiting us for the past week, conducting research. He's a foremost authority on MND, so I thought we should take advantage of his knowledge."

Dr. Meyers shook her hand. "Lovely to meet you, Julia."

Julia smiled at him weakly. "Well?"

Dr. Cavendish spread his hands open. "Inconclusive, I'm afraid. I think we're going to have to keep testing you every six months or so to see if we can definitely confirm MND or rule it out."

Julia slumped in her chair. Tears welled in her eyes. "I was hoping you'd say it was all just my imagination, and that I wasn't sick after all."

"No, I can see there's something there. We just can't be sure what yet. I was hoping my colleague here might be able to help, but he has confirmed what I thought. He did ask to meet on you, however."

Julia turned to Dr. Meyers. "Why?"

Dr. Meyers smiled. "The tests don't tell us everything. Sometimes just meeting a person tells us more. I must say you look good. Healthy."

"Yes," said Dr. Cavendish. "The holiday did her good. It might have been that which has caused this delay in a proper diagnosis."

Julia nodded. "I've been eating well too. And not drinking alcohol."

"Good. Sorry we can't give you a definitive answer, Julia." Dr. Cavendish stood. "Make an appointment for four or five months from now. If you feel dramatically worse in the meantime, come and see me sooner."

Julia walked out of the neurologist's office in a daze. She handed her credit card to Gail, with a weak smile, explaining that she'd need to come back in six months.

On the street, life went on as normal. People rushed up and down the footpaths, some talking into mobile telephones, others walking with heads bent as though looking for something lost. Julia stood still and watched the world for the longest time. She was waiting for her sense of confusion to fade.

CHAPTER TWENTY-SIX

Julia wondered why she hadn't thought of going to Raz's apartment first. Although her friend hadn't been staying there—she'd been at Julia's house—it would still be a bolt-hole in a time of distress. As she pulled up outside the apartment, she could see the door ajar, and was relieved to know Raz was there.

She knocked and pushed the door open gently. Raz was sitting at the dining table, her head lowered and her hands cupped on either side of her head. She looked up when Julia entered, and frowned. "Oh, hi."

"Hi to you too. I was worried. You didn't tell me you were going."

"I had to get away."

"Running never solved anything."

"I haven't gone far. If anyone wants to find me I'm right here."

Julia looked into Raz's eyes. They were different, somehow. Reminded Julia of another time, another Raz. The time before Julia went to Hong Kong.

Julia began moving from room to room, scouring Raz's apartment, opening bathroom cupboards and bedside tables. She moved into the kitchen and saw the packet on the sink.

She returned to the dining table with the tablets in her hand and sat down opposite Raz. She stared at her friend, unable to talk. Then the words came in a torrent.

"No Raz. No. Not drugs again. Jeez, how quickly did that happen?"

Raz's eyes didn't leave the table top. Julia reached over and shook her by the shoulders.

"No. No. Don't! Just don't! Would you really throw your life away again, after all that? Really—over a man? C'mon. You'd be the first to say how stupid that was. I'm really angry and disappointed in you, Raz."

Still her friend refused to look at her, remained mute.

"I thought we had something better than this, Raz. I thought you'd turn to me first, before taking that slide back down to hell. We're friends—more than friends." She took a deep breath and stood up. "If you're going to do that, I'm not going to stick around and watch you. You'll be on your own. You can't know how much you've disappointed me."

That made her friend look up. "You don't get it, do you? It's you. It's always you. Always has been and always will be. It's not only that I'm losing Steve..." She began sobbing.

"What do you mean? What are you saying?"

"Right from the start, when we were at school. Right from the first day when you took me home. You fed me and looked after me. Your Mum didn't like me much, but she protected me. You became my family. I don't think you ever really understood that."

Julia breathed deeply and took Raz's hands, but she snatched them back.

"You know, it's like a puppy that's been kicked and starved. One day it's rescued by the best human being in the world who treats it with love and respect. That puppy will be loyal to that person to the end of time. To the death. That's me and you. You saved me. I don't know what would've happened without you. Those nights I came and slept on your floor..." She was sobbing and hiccoughing. "You saved me and we had wonderful times together. I was so happy. You were my new family. Then you met George and had the boys, and your attention went away a bit. But that was okay, sort of. I had to cope with that. But then you went to Hong Kong, and I felt like I was dying."

"You nearly did die."

"I thought I'd lost you. Thought you'd gone for good. But you came back and we were happy again. For ages. Set up the coffee shop and all that. Then Peter came. It was worse that time. You shut me out." Raz's voice went dead when she said those words.

"I'm so sorry Raz. You know that."

"He made you buy me out of the coffee shop. Hated me being around you. You didn't know, but when you weren't around, or even when you were just out of earshot, he was rude to me. I felt like stabbing him, I was so angry."

"Can't say I blame you."

"The worst part, the very worst part, was I could see he didn't love you and that was truly catastrophic for me. Watching you waste yourself on that prick."

The women sat in silence. Raz was catching her breath. "I went really bad. You didn't know. Drugs again and other things. You weren't around and, I had to pull myself out of it. Found a great therapist."

"I'm so sorry." Julia was whispering.

"And then snap! Christopher contacts me and says you're in trouble. You won't tell anyone what's wrong. You need me. There I am, back with you and the lights come on again. The sun shines. The world is full of colour. Then you *tell me you might be dying!*" These last words come out as a primal scream. "*Dying! You?*" Raz pulled a sleeve across her nose. "When you told me that, I just wanted to curl up and die with you."

Julia tried to interrupt, but her friend kept talking over her. "Then all of a sudden there's Steve. I know that I will go through a bad time if you're taken from me, but then Steve would've make it okay. I thought the universe was being unusually kind, had sent someone to save me. So I thought. Now he's abandoning me too." Raz rested her head on her arms and sobbed.

Julia reached for Raz's hands again. "Well, there's a couple of things you ought to know right away. Firstly, I don't think Steve's leaving you at all. He's just been placed in a bad situation and doesn't want to dump the girl cruelly. Men are weak, Raz. But he'll sort it out. I'm sure of it. I've seen you and him together and it's just magic. It isn't the same between him and the Irish girl. Give him a couple of days."

Raz raised her head. Her eyes were bloodshot. "Do you really think that? You're not just saying it?"

"No, it's true. And when he sorts it all out and you're together again, you should tell him."

"Tell him what?"

"He needs to understand why you have certain…issues. Tell him about your past—what happened to you that was so bad you could never bring yourself to even open up to me about it."

"That's funny coming from the queen of secrets!"

"But I've never been as lucky as you—to have a man like Steve. He is special. He's totally non-judgmental. It will bring the two of you even closer together."

"Maybe."

"It's true. But that's not all. The next thing you should know is that I got some calls about Peter today. A miracle. He wants Sylvia to look after him. Thanks, Raz." Her friend shrugged.

"But there's even more. I saved the best until last. The neurologist—I saw him this afternoon—he can't confirm I have MND."

"What?" Raz sat straighter in her chair. "Really?"

"True. I might have, but the tests are inconclusive. I have to go back in five months. I don't have a death sentence yet, darling Raz." Julia wiped her eyes. "But if it ends up that I do have it, I'm going to need you. Really need you. See, you are my family, too. I know what you're saying about how things were at school and home for you, and how you think I saved you, but you've saved me, too. The whole thing with the baby. You were always so protective of me." Julia smiled and ran her fingers through Raz's hair. "It's always been you, too. You and I have an amazing friendship. And we will continue to have it and nobody will come between us again. Ever."

Julia watched the light come on in Raz's eyes again. Her friend was going to be all right.

"So, put on some fancy clothes, darling Raz. Let's go out and celebrate something. Life. A reprieve. A great friendship. I might even have a night off the veggies and allow myself a glass of champagne. How's that?"

At last Raz's cocky smile was back. "Alright!"

Julia was in the living room, pacing, listening to the voices flowing in from the back deck. Everybody was eating and drinking, but in a subdued way. They were unsure why they had been summoned.

From time to time she'd look through the window at them and her stomach would squeeze. She wished she hadn't decided on this course of action—wished she'd just spoken to them individually. Deep down, however, she knew this was the best way.

Emilie was standing in the corner of the deck with Guy and little Isabel. Steve was keeping them company, making sure they didn't feel out of place, telling them a long story in his lovely accent. Raz came to the window and signaled to her. It was time.

She walked through the French windows and onto the deck. Nicholas walked up to her quickly. "Hey, Mum. Who are those people from France? She's beautiful!"

Julia smiled. "You're just about to find out."

Raz tapped her glass with a fork and, as the small group fell silent, gave Julia the thumbs-up.

"Hi everyone. I guess you're wondering why you're here—why I invited you..." Her voice faded. Amanda, standing near the back, nodded encouragingly.

Julia cleared her throat. "A lot has happened since I flew back into Australia, and I've been so busy just trying to put out fires that I've neglected some important duties. I've seen you all and have spoken to you, but I haven't really communicated everything very well. I know some of you have been angry at me for going away suddenly, and this has been fuelled by my keeping things secret." She saw her mother and father nodding. Costas still wore the hostile look he had when he collected her from the airport.

"I guess I'm a bit secretive by nature. At least I've been accused of that. I now see how destructive and cruel that has been to those I love and I plan to remedy that." She saw her father begin to smile.

"Gosh, where do I start? Let's jump in the deep end. See that beautiful woman over there in the corner? That's Emilie. She is standing with her husband Guy and daughter Isabel. It's time you all met her because— she is my daughter." There was a collective gasp. Julia felt tears welling in her eyes. She swallowed hard. "I gave her up for adoption when I was only eighteen. In France."

Julia saw a look of great happiness cross Nicholas's face. "A sister! Wow!" He went and stood beside Emilie and smiled at her.

"So, one of the reasons I went overseas was to see Emilie for the first time since she was born. The decision to do this—the reason I did it so suddenly, was..." Her voice failed again. Raz came and stood beside her, and put an arm around her shoulders. "Was because I discovered I might have a serious health problem." She saw her mother frown. "I went to France before...well while I still could, and before anybody could try to change my mind. Emilie and I went to a remote part of the French coast for a week where there is no mobile telephone reception. That's why nobody could contact me." There was murmuring around the group.

"I should tell you now, quickly, that I have had tests and they are inconclusive. I don't know if I have this condition or not, and won't for at least several months. If I'm found to be suffering from it, I'll need all your love and support."

Julia's mother was looking pale. "What is it—this health problem?"

"I wasn't going to specify the disorder. Seems premature. But if you must know, it is Motor Neurone Disease."

Julia's mother was sobbing into Julia's father's chest. Christopher looked like the end of the world was nigh. Costas was pale and visibly shaking.

"I can't blame any of you for thinking the worst when I disappeared like that. As you all reminded me, I'd done it before. I've been bad in the past, but all of that has changed." Julia paused. "There are a couple more things to tell you. Peter is returning to his wife and daughters when he leaves hospital. I agree with this decision, and it seems to be the best for all concerned." There was a look of puzzlement on several of the faces. Julia hurried on. "I plan to spend quite some time with Emilie, Guy and Isabel in the future. If you can't find me, look in France." There was general laughter. "Raz and Steve here will be running the café while I'm gone. They've got great ideas for the business, and that's why I've taken them on as partners. The great news, and they only told me this today, is that they plan to get married soon." Julia saw Christopher walk around the back of the group to congratulate them and she realised that Raz and Steve would never have met if Christopher hadn't brought her and Raz together again. She had a thought then, about how fragile happiness is. How you must grasp it and hang on tight.

Julia looked down at her feet and cleared her throat. "The main thing I wanted to say to you all is this. I have, just very recently, come to understand the terrible price of secrets—how dangerous and corrosive they are to relationships. Today I swear there will be no more secrets between me and those I love."

Nicholas ran over and flung himself into Julia's arms. She stroked his hair.

Everybody crowded around her then—all the people she loved. They took turns to hug her, reassure her. Julia's mother held her daughter fiercely, unable to talk. Then she disengaged and turned away, wiping her nose with a tissue. She greeted Emilie who had been waiting patiently to meet her grandmother.

Somebody tapped Julia on the shoulder. She turned to see Christopher looking at her with a cheeky grin. "Look who I've got with me." She turned further to see the flirty lawyer, Damien, smiling at her. "I hope you don't mind me inviting him. I didn't realise it was going to be such an emotional event."

"No, of course I don't mind." She turned to the lawyer. "I hope you're looking after Christopher well. It must be a difficult case."

"Oh, yes. I'm looking after Chris very well." The two men began laughing. Julia watched their interplay carefully, and the truth dawned. That's why Christopher had never been able to keep a girlfriend. She wondered what her parents would think. At least the spotlight would be off her for a while.

Raz stood back through all of this, holding Steve's hand. At last, Julia was standing apart from the others again. Raz walked over, a cocky walk with attitude, just like the old Raz, the teenage one.

Julia smiled at her. "Raz, my wonderful friend."

"I told Steve, a couple of days ago."

"About what?"

"Me. My therapist agreed with you that I should tell Steve about—well—about my past."

Julia's smile was soft. "So, what was Steven's reaction?"

"When I started to tell him, he took me into the

bedroom and lay me down. He spooned into my back and began stroking my hair. He told me to tell him everything."

"And?"

"I talked and talked. Do you know he didn't interrupt once? He just held me until all the words were used up, all the crying done. Then he asked me just a few questions that made me realise that he understood totally and on a very deep level. We spoke about the importance of forgiveness, or at least acceptance. We spoke about how much I had to be grateful for in my life and how the events of my past, as bad as they were, have shaped me into who I am today and how he loves that person."

"He has an advanced soul, that man."

"He has, absolutely. And that's why we've decided to get married. We're just so confident that we know each other totally."

Julia hugged her friend. "You deserve all of this. To be happy with the best man on earth. I'm quite jealous, you know."

"No need to be. You're free of Peter now. You can find a good man."

"Oh, of course! Just snap my fingers and there he'll be. My soul-mate."

Raz began jiggling on the spot. "I know him. Know who it is!"

"What? What are you talking about?"

"A mate of Steven's. Lives near the New South Wales border. We visited him a couple of weekends ago, and I remember thinking how good you two would be together."

Julia laughed. "Trust you to think you could arrange the perfect man for me. In reality, I can't take on anyone new until I sort out this health issue."

"Why?"

"You know why. I meet someone, we fall in love, and then I'm diagnosed with a terminal disease. How bad would that be?"

"It wouldn't matter with this guy. Even if you had the disease. He just lives one day at a time, and he's so accepting of everything. Great guy."

"Thanks. I really appreciate the thought, but not just yet."

"Okay, but sometimes you just have to grab stuff—the good stuff in life—while it's on offer. Perfect moments don't just appear when you want them to."

"I promise I'll give it some thought."

"He'll be here next weekend, anyway. At least meet the guy. Pauric is his name."

"Maybe. I'll let you know." Julia knew she was wasting her breath. If her friend had decided that Pauric was the ideal man, there would be no stopping her.

Rachel changed the subject. "Hey. I was thinking—while you were making that speech..."

"What about?"

"I was thinking how they should make a movie about us. About you and me."

"Why?"

"Because we're worth knowing about. It's like "Beaches", or "Thelma and Louise" although we don't drive over a cliff."

Julia laughed. Raz could always make her feel good. "Well, okay. What would it be called, this movie? Oh, you're a writer now. You could write our story—the screenplay."

"Yeah. Definitely. As for a name, gee, you've put me on the spot." She put a finger to her cheek and looked skywards. "Hey, I've got it!"

"Okay, tell me."

"I'd call it, "An Uncommon Friendship."

Julia squeezed Raz's arm. "Yes, that's perfect. That really sums up what you and I have. An uncommon friendship indeed."

Thank you for reading "The Secrets of Julia Hawke". Reviews are important to authors, so if you take time to give honest feedback on Amazon.com, this would be appreciated.

If you enjoyed the book, please tell your friends.

If you would like updates on future publications by Brenda Cheers, please 'like' the **Brenda Cheers-Author** Facebook page:
http://on.fb.me/1wXszz1

ACKNOWLEDGEMENTS

To those who read my drafts and give advice, thank you again—Bex, Terry, Tracey, June and Robyn. This is always greatly appreciated.

Writing is essentially a solo journey. Sometimes, when immersed in my stories, I neglect those closest to me. I would like to thank those people for their patience and lack of complaint.

Where would I be without my loyal readers? You buy my books. Wow. Some of you become fans on Goodreads while others send messages of support. What can I say? You are my best friends. Bless you.

Brenda Cheers lives in Brisbane, Australia with her partner and two daughters.

"The Secrets of Julia Hawke" is her sixth published novel.

Visit www.brendacheersbooks.com for further information.

Also by Brenda Cheers

Coming
2015

In Strange
Worlds
#3